William Shakespeare's 3 Henry VI, aka Henry VI, Part 3: A Retelling in Prose

David Bruce

Published by David Bruce, 2022.

WILLIAM SHAKESPEARE'S 3 HENRY VI, AKA HENRY VI, PART 3: A RETELLING IN PROSE

First edition. July 26, 2022.

Copyright © 2022 David Bruce.

ISBN: 979-8201578145

Written by David Bruce.

Table of Contents

Dedication

DEDICATED TO MY SISTER MARTHA

Martha wrote, "When I was working at Longaberger, I worked with a girl who had two children and was in the middle of a divorce. She was so worried about Christmas for her boys. I received a very nice Christmas bonus that year, and I went to my boss and started a donation fund for the girl. My boss told me later that she — my boss —delivered the money to the girl's mother and father and told them not to tell her who brought the money for her. Months later the girl told me that the boys had the best Christmas that year, and she told me someone had brought money to her mom and dad for her, and she went to town and bought the boys Christmas. She never did know who did that for her. She was so thankful. I believe that I was the only one who donated to her, which was just fine."

***

The doing of good deeds is important. As a free person, you can choose to live your life as a good person or as a bad person. To be a good person, do good deeds. To be a bad person, do bad deeds. If you do good deeds, you will become good. If you do bad deeds, you will become bad. To become the person you want to be, act as if you already are that kind of person. Each of us chooses what kind of person we will become. To become a good person, do the things a good person does. To become a bad person, do the things a bad person does. The opportunity to take action to become the kind of person you want to be is yours.

Educate Yourself
Read Like A Wolf Eats
Be Excellent to Each Other
Books Then, Books Now, Books Forever

***

In this retelling, as in all my retellings, I have tried to make the work of literature accessible to modern readers who may lack the knowledge about mythology, religion, and history that the literary work's contemporary audience had.

Do you know a language other than English? If you do, I give you permission to translate this book, copyright your translation, publish or self-publish it, and keep all the royalties for yourself. (Do give me credit, of course, for the original retelling.)

I would like to see my retellings of classic literature used in schools, so I give permission to the country of Finland (and all other countries) to give copies of this book to all students forever. I also give permission to the state of Texas (and all other states) to give copies of this book to all students forever. I also give permission to all teachers to give copies of this book to all students forever.

Teachers need not actually teach my retellings. Teachers are welcome to give students copies of my eBooks as background material. For example, if they are teaching Homer's *Iliad* and *Odyssey*, teachers are welcome to give students copies of my *Virgil's* Aeneid: *A Retelling in Prose* and tell students, "Here's another ancient epic you may want to read in your spare time."

CAST OF CHARACTERS

Male Characters

King Henry VI.

Edward, Prince of Wales, King Henry VI's son.

Louis XI, King of France.

Duke of Somerset. At the end of *2 Henry VI*, the then Duke of Somerset is killed; at the beginning of *3 Henry VI*, Richard is holding his severed head. This Duke of Somerset is the son of the earlier Duke of Somerset.

Duke of Exeter.

Earl of Oxford.

Earl of Northumberland.

Earl of Westmoreland.

Lord Clifford. This is the young Clifford of *2 Henry VI*. His father was killed near the end of *2 Henry VI*.

Richard Plantagenet, Duke of York.

Edward, Earl of March, afterwards King Edward IV, York's son.

Edmund, Earl of Rutland, York's son.

George, afterwards Duke of Clarence, York's son.

Richard, afterwards Duke of Gloucester, York's son; later, he becomes King Richard III.

Duke of Norfolk.

Marquess of Montague, the Earl of Warwick's brother and the Duke of York's nephew. The Duke of York and the Marquess of Montague sometimes call each other "brother" as a term of affection.

Earl of Warwick.

Earl of Pembroke.

Lord Hastings.

Lord Stafford.

Sir John Mortimer and Sir Hugh Mortimer, uncles to the Duke of York.

Henry, Earl of Richmond, a youth; later, he becomes King Henry VII. As King Henry VII, he will end the Wars of the Roses and will begin the Tudor Dynasty. He is a Yorkist, but he will marry a Lancastrian.

Lord Rivers, brother to Lady Elizabeth Grey.

Sir William Stanley.

Sir John Montgomery.

Sir John Somerville.

Tutor to Rutland.

Mayor of York.

Lieutenant of the Tower.

A Nobleman.

Two Gamekeepers.

A Huntsman.

A Son who has killed his father.

A Father who has killed his son.

Female Characters

Queen Margaret.

Lady Elizabeth Grey, afterwards Queen consort to Edward IV.

Lady Bona, sister to the French Queen.

Minor Characters

Soldiers, Attendants, Messengers, Watchmen, etc.

SCENE

England.

NOTA BENE

Lancastrians and Yorkists

King Henry VI is a Lancastrian; he is the Duke of Lancaster as well as the King of England.

The symbol of the Lancastrians is a red rose.

The Duke of York is a Yorkist.

The symbol of the Yorkists is a white rose.

The roses were worn in hats.

Lancastrians

King Henry VI.

Edward, Prince of Wales.

Earl of Oxford.

Earl of Northumberland.

Lord Clifford.

Sir John Somerville.

Queen Margaret.

Yorkists

The Duke of York.

Edward, Earl of March, afterwards King Edward IV, York's son.

Edmund, Earl of Rutland, York's son.

Richard, afterwards Duke of Gloucester, York's son; later, he becomes King Richard III.

Sir John Mortimer, uncle to the Duke of York.

Sir Hugh Mortimer, uncle to the Duke of York.

Duke of Norfolk.

Earl of Pembroke.

Lord Hastings.

Lord Stafford.

Lord Rivers.

Sir John Montgomery.

Tutor to Rutland.

Lady Elizabeth Grey.

Side Switchers

The Earl of Warwick switches from the Yorkist to the Lancastrian side.

The Marquess of Montague switches from the Yorkist to the Lancastrian side.

At the beginning of Chapter 4, the Duke of Somerset is at the court of the Lancastrian King Edward IV, but he leaves join the Lancastrian side.

George, afterwards Duke of Clarence, the Duke of York's son, at first is a Yorkist, but then he switches allegiance to the Lancastrians, and then he switches allegiance back to the Yorkists.

House of York, House of Lancaster

In this context, the word "House" means "Family."

History and Literature

The Hundred Years War, which lasted from 1337-1453 (116 years), was not fought continuously. The Edwardian War took place in 1337-1360; the Caroline War took place in 1369-1389; the Lancastrian War took place in 1415-1453.

After the Hundred Years War, the Wars of the Roses took place from 1455-1487. In those wars, the Yorkists and the Lancastrians fought for power in England. The emblem of the York family was a white rose, and the emblem of the Lancaster family was a red rose.

We read Shakespeare for drama, not history. He invents scenes and changes the ages of historical personages in his plays. He also changes the order in which historical events occur.

CHAPTER 1

—1.1 —

The Duke of York, his sons Edward and Richard, as well as the Duke of Norfolk, the Marquess of Montague, and the Earl of Warwick entered the Parliament House in London. With them were some soldiers. They were wearing white roses, the symbol of the House of York.

The Earl of Warwick said, "I wonder how King Henry VI escaped our hands."

The Duke of York said, "While we pursued the horsemen of the north, he slyly stole away and left his men. At that time the great Lord of Northumberland, whose soldierly ears could never endure the call to retreat, rallied the drooping army, and he himself, old Lord Clifford, and Lord Stafford, all abreast, charged our main army's front lines, and after breaking through were slain by the swords of common soldiers."

Actually, the Duke of York had himself killed old Lord Clifford, but he was insulting old Lord Clifford and the other two enemies by claiming that common soldiers had killed them. According to the protocol of chivalry, an honorable death for nobles in battle could occur only if nobles killed other nobles.

Edward said, "Lord Stafford's father, the Duke of Buckingham, is either slain or dangerously wounded. I cleft his beaver — part of the face guard of his helmet — with a downward blow. So that you know this is true, father, behold his blood."

Edward lifted his bloody sword.

The Marquess of Montague said, "And, brother, here's the Earl of Wiltshire's blood, whom I encountered as the armies met and fought."

The Marquess of Montague was the Earl of Warwick's brother and the Duke of York's nephew.

Richard said to the bloody head — that of the Duke of Somerset — he was holding, "Speak for me and tell them what I did."

Richard's father, the Duke of York, said, "Richard has best deserved of all my sons."

The Duke of Somerset had been one of the Duke of York's greatest enemies.

The Duke of York then said to the bloody head, "But is your grace dead, my Lord of Somerset?"

The Duke of Norfolk said, "May all the line of John of Gaunt have such hope! May all of them end up dead!"

John of Gaunt had been the Duke of Lancaster, and now his descendants, the Lancastrians, including King Henry VI, were fighting a war against the Yorkists, who were led by the Duke of York.

Richard said, "Thus do I hope to shake King Henry VI's head."

He shook the Duke of Somerset's head and then threw it on the floor.

"And so do I," the Earl of Warwick said. "Victorious Prince of York, before I see you seated in that throne that now the House of Lancaster usurps, I vow by Heaven these eyes shall never close. This is the palace of the timid, frightened King Henry VI, and this is the regal seat."

He pointed to the throne.

He then said, "Possess it, Duke of York, for this is your throne. It does not belong to the heirs of King Henry IV."

"Assist me, then, sweet Warwick, and I will," the Duke of York said, "for we have broken in here by force."

"We'll all assist you," the Duke of Norfolk said. "Any man who flees shall die."

"Thanks, noble Norfolk," the Duke of York said. "Stay by me, my lords.

"And, soldiers, stay and lodge by me this night."

The Duke of York and his relatives and close allies approached the throne, and the soldiers hid themselves.

The Earl of Warwick said, "And when the King comes, offer him no violence, unless he should seek to thrust you out by force."

"Queen Margaret holds her Parliament here this day," the Duke of York said. "But she little thinks we shall be part of her council. By words or blows, here let us win our right."

"Armed as we are, let's stay within this house," Richard said.

"This shall be called the Bloody Parliament," the Earl of Warwick said, "unless Plantagenet, Duke of York, becomes King, and easily intimidated Henry VI is deposed — Henry VI, whose cowardice has made us objects of scorn to our enemies. According to our enemies, we are bywords — notorious examples — of cowardice."

"Then don't leave me, my lords," the Duke of York said. "Be resolute. I mean to take possession of my right; I am the rightful King of England."

The Earl of Warwick said, "Neither King Henry VI, nor the man who loves him best, the proudest and bravest man who holds up and supports Lancaster, will dare to stir a wing, if I, Warwick, should shake my bells."

He was referring metaphorically to the bells that were tied to the legs of a falcon. In this culture, people believed that the falcon's prey was frightened when hearing the bells.

The Earl of Warwick continued, "I'll plant Plantagenet, and root up anyone who dares to oppose him. Resolve yourself, Duke Richard of York, to claim the English crown."

The Duke of York sat on the throne.

Trumpets sounded, and King Henry VI, Lord Clifford, the Earl of Northumberland, the Earl of Westmoreland, the Duke of Exeter, and others entered the room. They were wearing red roses, the symbol of the House of Lancaster.

Seeing the Duke of York sitting on the throne, King Henry VI said, "My lords, look where the sturdy rebel sits, even on the throne — the chair of state. Probably he intends, backed by the power of the Earl of Warwick, that false peer, to aspire to the crown and reign as King.

"Earl of Northumberland, the Duke of York slew your father. Lord Clifford, the Duke of York also slew your father. Both of you have vowed revenge on him, his sons, his followers, and his friends."

"If I be not revenged on him, may the Heavens be revenged on me!" the Earl of Northumberland swore.

"The hope of getting revenge makes me, Clifford, mourn while wearing steel armor," Lord Clifford said.

"Shall we endure this?" the Earl of Westmoreland said. "Let's pluck the Duke of York down from his seat on the throne. My heart burns because of my anger; I cannot endure it."

"Be patient, noble Earl of Westmoreland," King Henry VI said.

Lord Clifford said, "Patience is for cowardly poltroons, such as the Duke of York. He would not dare to sit there, if your father, Henry V, had lived. My gracious lord, here in the Parliament let us assail the family of York."

"Well have you spoken, kinsman," the Earl of Northumberland said. "Be it so. Let's do it."

"Ah, don't you know that the citizens of London favor them," King Henry VI said, "and that they have troops of soldiers at their beck and call?"

"But when the Duke of York is slain, his troops will quickly flee," the Duke of Exeter said.

"Far be from my, Henry's, heart the thought of making a shambles — a meat market, a slaughterhouse — of the Parliament House," King Henry VI said. "Kinsman of Exeter, frowns, words, and threats shall be the weapons of war that Henry means to use.

"You factious Duke of York, descend from my throne, and kneel for grace and mercy at my feet. I am your sovereign. I am your King."

"I am yours," the Duke of York said.

"For shame, come down," the Duke of Exeter said. "Henry VI made you Duke of York."

"The Dukedom was my inheritance, as the Earldom was," the Duke of York said.

He had also inherited the title of Earl of March.

"Your father was a traitor to the crown, and so your Dukedom was given to you, and not inherited by you," the Duke of Exeter said. Your father lost his title and lands because of his treason."

"Exeter, you are a traitor to the crown in following this usurping Henry VI," the Duke of Warwick said.

"Whom should he follow but his natural King?" Lord Clifford said.

The word "natural" means "legitimate, rightful, by birthright."

"What you said is true, Clifford," the Earl of Warwick said. "He should follow his natural King, and that is Richard, Duke of York."

King Henry VI said, "And shall I stand, and you sit on my throne?"

"It must and shall be so," the Duke of York said. "Content yourself. Be calm and accept it."

The Earl of Warwick said to Henry VI, "Be Duke of Lancaster; let him be King."

The Earl of Westmoreland said, "King Henry VI is both King of England and Duke of Lancaster, and that the Lord of Westmoreland shall maintain. Henry VI is my King."

"And I, Warwick, shall disprove it," the Earl of Warwick said. "You forget that we are those who chased you from the battlefield and slew your fathers, and with our battle flags unfurled, we marched through the city to the palace gates."

"Yes, Warwick, I remember it to my grief," the Earl of Northumberland said. "And, by my father's soul, you and your House shall rue it."

The Earl of Westmoreland said to the Duke of York, "Plantagenet, of you and these your sons, your kinsmen, and your friends, I'll have more lives than drops of blood that were in my father's veins."

"Do not keep reminding me about the death of my father," Lord Clifford said, "lest that, instead of words, I send you, Warwick, such a messenger as shall revenge his death before I stir."

A basilisk can kill without stirring — moving. Merely seeing this mythological serpent kills. Another messenger of death from afar is an arrow. Yet another messenger of death is an exterminating angel.

"Poor Clifford!" the Earl of Warwick said. "How I scorn his worthless threats!"

Future events would show that Lord Clifford could kill important enemies.

Using the royal plural, the Duke of York said to King Henry VI, "Do you want us to show you the truth of our rightful title to the crown? If not, our swords in the battlefield shall plead my right to the crown."

"What title do you, traitor, have to the crown?" King Henry VI said. "Your father was, as you are, Duke of York. Your grandfather was Roger Mortimer, the Earl of March.

"I am the son of King Henry V, who forced the Dauphin and the French to stoop in submission and who captured their towns and provinces."

The Dauphin claimed to be King of France, but King Henry V of England disputed that claim.

"Don't talk about France," the Earl of Warwick said, "since you have lost it all."

"The Lord Protector, not I, lost it. When I was crowned King of England, I was only nine months old."

"You are old enough now, and yet, I think, you continue to lose," Richard said.

He added, "Father, tear the crown from the usurper's head."

"Sweet father, do so," Edward said. "Set it on your head."

The Marquess of Montague said to the Duke of York, "Good brother, as you love and honor arms, let's fight it out and not stand here disputing over details like this."

Richard said, "If the drums and trumpets start playing, King Henry VI will flee."

"Sons, peace!" the Duke of York said.

"Peace, all of you!" King Henry VI said. "Give King Henry the opportunity to speak."

"Plantagenet — the Duke of York — shall speak first," the Earl of Warwick said. "Hear him, lords."

He then said to King Henry VI, "And be you silent and attentive, too, for he who interrupts the Duke of York shall not live."

"Do you think that I will leave my Kingly throne, in which my grandfather and my father sat?" King Henry VI said. "No. Before that happens, war shall depopulate this — my — realm. Yes, and their battle flags, often borne in France, and now borne in England to our heart's great sorrow, shall be my winding-sheet — my shroud."

He said to his supporters, "Why are you losing courage, lords? My title to the crown is good, and far better than his."

"Prove it, Henry," the Earl of Warwick said, "and you shall be King."

"My grandfather, Henry IV, got the crown," King Henry VI said.

"It was by rebellion against his King," the Duke of York objected.

This is true. King Henry IV had forced King Richard II to abdicate as King.

King Henry VI thought, *I don't know what to say; my claim to the crown is weak.*

He said out loud, "Tell me, may not a King adopt an heir?"

"What of it?" the Duke of York asked.

"If he may, then I am your lawful King," King Henry VI said. "For King Richard II, in the presence of many lords, resigned the crown to King Henry IV, whose heir my father was, and I am his."

"Henry IV rose against Richard II, who was his sovereign," the Duke of York said, "and by force made him resign his crown."

"Suppose, my lords, that Richard II resigned the crown without being constrained," the Earl of Warwick said. "Do you think it would be prejudicial to the Duke of York's claim to the crown?"

"No," the Duke of Exeter whispered to King Henry VI, "for Richard II could not so resign his crown unless the next heir should succeed him and reign as King. The crown must pass to the next in line to be King."

Shocked at hearing this from a man whom he considered to a supporter, King Henry VI whispered to him, "Are you against us, Duke of Exeter?"

"The Duke of York is in the right, and therefore pardon me," the Duke of Exeter whispered.

King Henry VI's claim to the crown rested on his being descended from John of Gaunt, Duke of Lancaster, who was the fourth son of King Edward III.

The Duke of York's claim to the throne rested on his being descended from Lionel, Duke of Clarence, who was the third son of King Edward III. However, his line of descent included males and a female, while Henry VI's line of descent included only males.

The Duke of York asked, "Why are you whispering among yourselves, my lords, and not answering me?"

"My conscience tells me that the Duke of York is the lawful King of England," the Duke of Exeter whispered.

King Henry VI thought, *Everyone will revolt from me, and everyone will turn to the Duke of York.*

The Earl of Northumberland said to the Duke of York, "Plantagenet, for all the claim to the crown you are making, don't think that King Henry VI shall be so deposed."

"Deposed he shall be, in spite of all," the Earl of Warwick said.

"You are deceived," the Earl of Northumberland said. "It is not your southern power of Essex, Norfolk, Suffolk, or of Kent — which makes you thus presumptuous and proud — that can set the Duke of York on the throne in spite — contemptuous dismissal — of me."

Lord Clifford whispered, "King Henry VI, whether your claim to the throne is right or wrong, I, Lord Clifford, vow to fight in your defense. May that ground gape and swallow me alive, if and where I would kneel to that man who slew my father!"

Numbers 16:30 states, "*But if the Lord make a new thing, and the earth open her mouth, and swallow them up with all that they have, and they go down quick into the pit: then ye shall understand that these men have provoked the Lord*" (1599 Geneva Bible).

King Henry VI whispered, "Oh, Clifford, how your words revive my heart!"

The Duke of York said, "Henry of Lancaster, resign your crown. What are you muttering, or what are you conspiring, lords?"

The Earl of Warwick said, "Do right to this Princely Duke of York, or I will fill the house with armed men, and over the chair of state — the throne — where now he sits, I will write up his title with the blood of the usurper."

He stamped with his foot and the soldiers who had been hidden showed themselves.

"My Lord of Warwick, hear me speak but one word," King Henry VI said. "Let me for my lifetime reign as King."

The Duke of York said, "Confirm the crown to me and to my heirs, and you shall reign in quiet while you live. But after you die, I will reign and after I die, my heirs will reign."

"I am content," King Henry VI said. "I agree. Richard Plantagenet, Duke of York, enjoy the Kingdom after my decease."

Lord Clifford objected to the decision: "What a wrong is this to the Prince, your son!"

The Earl of Warwick approved of the decision: "What good is this to England and to Henry VI himself!"

The Earl of Westmoreland objected to the decision: "Base, dishonorable, frightened, and despairing Henry!"

Lord Clifford said, "How you have injured both yourself and us!"

The Earl of Westmoreland said, "I cannot stay to hear these legal articles that you two — York and Henry — will draw up between yourselves."

"Nor can I," the Earl of Northumberland said.

"Come, cousin, let us tell Queen Margaret the news," Lord Clifford said.

The Earl of Westmoreland said, "Farewell, faint-hearted and degenerate King Henry VI, in whose cold, hopeless blood no spark of honor abides."

The Earl of Northumberland said to King Henry VI, "May you be a prey for the House of York, and die wearing shackles for this unmanly deed of yours!"

Lord Clifford said to the King, "May you be overcome in dreadful war, or live abandoned and despised in peace!"

The Earl of Westmoreland, the Earl of Northumberland, and Lord Clifford exited.

King Henry VI watched them go.

The Earl of Warwick said, "Turn this way, Henry VI, and pay no attention to them."

The Duke of Exeter said, "They seek revenge and therefore will not yield."

"Ah, Exeter!" King Henry VI said.

"Why should you sigh, my lord?" the Earl of Warwick asked.

"I sigh not for myself, Lord Warwick, but for my son, whom I unnaturally and not like a father shall disinherit. But be it as it may."

He said to the Duke of York, "I here entail the crown to you and to your heirs forever, on this condition, that here you take an oath to stop this civil war, and to honor me as your King and sovereign while I live, and neither by treason nor by hostility to seek to put me down and reign as King yourself."

"This oath I willingly take and will perform," the Duke of York said.

"Long live King Henry VI!" the Earl of Warwick said. "Plantagenet, embrace him."

King Henry VI climbed up onto the platform on which the throne was placed, the Duke of York stood up, and King Henry VI and the Duke of York embraced.

King Henry VI said, "And long may you and your promising sons live!"

"Now York and the Duke of Lancaster — you, Henry — are reconciled," the Duke of York said.

"May any man who seeks to make them foes be cursed!" the Duke of Exeter said.

"Farewell, my gracious lord," the Duke of York said. "I'll go to my castle."

"And I'll stay in London with my soldiers," the Earl of Warwick said.

"And I will go to Norfolk with my followers," the Duke of Norfolk said.

"And I will go to the sea from whence I came," the Marquess of Montague said.

Everyone exited except King Henry VI and the Duke of Exeter and a few attendants.

King Henry VI said, "And I, with grief and sorrow, will go to the court."

Queen Margaret and Edward, Prince of Wales, entered the room.

The Duke of Exeter said, "Here comes the Queen, whose looks reveal her anger. I'll steal away."

"Exeter, so will I," King Henry VI said.

Too late.

Queen Margaret said to her husband, King Henry VI, "No, don't go away from me! I will follow you!"

"Be patient and calm, my gentle, noble Queen, and I will stay," King Henry VI said.

"Who can be patient in such extreme times?" Queen Margaret said. "Ah, wretched man! I wish that I had died a virgin maiden and never seen you, never borne you a son, seeing you have proven to be so unnatural a father. Has your son, the Prince of Wales, deserved to lose his birthright thus? Had you loved him only half as well as I do, or felt that pain which I did for him once in childbirth, or nourished him as I did with my blood *in utero*, you would have left your dearest heart-blood there, rather than have made that savage Duke of York your heir and disinherited your only son."

"Father, you cannot disinherit me," Prince Edward said. "If you are the King, why shouldn't I succeed you as King?"

"Pardon me, Margaret; pardon me, sweet son," King Henry VI said. "The Earl of Warwick and the Duke of York forced me."

"Forced you!" Margaret said. "Are you King, and you will be forced? I am ashamed to hear you speak. Ah, timorous wretch! You have ruined yourself, your son, and me, and you have given to the House of York such power and strength that you shall reign only by their permission.

"To entail the crown to the Duke of York and his heirs, what is it but to make your sepulcher and creep into it far before your time?"

In this culture, people believed that the loss of a King's life quickly followed the loss of his power.

Queen Margaret continued, "Warwick is Chancellor and the lord of Calais. Stern Falconbridge commands the narrow seas. The Duke of York has been made Lord Protector of the realm. And yet you shall be safe? Such safety finds the trembling lamb surrounded by wolves.

"Had I been there, I who am a defenseless woman, the soldiers would have impaled and carried me aloft on their pikes before I would have agreed to that act of Parliament which gives your enemies all that power.

"But you preferred your life before your honor, and seeing that you do, I here divorce myself, Henry, both from your table and your bed until that act of Parliament by which my son is disinherited is repealed.

"The northern lords who have forsworn your battle flags will follow mine, if once they see them unfurled, and unfurled they shall be, to your foul disgrace and the utter ruin of the House of York.

"Thus I leave you.

"Come, son, let's leave. Our army is ready. Come, we'll go after our enemies."

"Stay, gentle, noble Margaret, and hear me speak," King Henry VI said.

"You have spoken too much already," Queen Maragret said. "Get you gone! Get lost!"

"Gentle son Edward, will you stay with me?" King Henry VI asked.

Queen Margaret said to her son, Prince Edward, "If you do, you will be murdered by your enemies."

Prince Edward said, "When I return with victory from the battlefield, I'll see your grace. Until then I'll follow her."

"Come, son, let's go," Queen Margaret said. "We cannot waste time here."

Queen Margaret and Prince Edward exited.

King Henry VI said, "Poor Queen! How her love for me and for her son has made her break out into terms of rage! Revenged may she be on that hateful Duke of York, whose haughty spirit, winged with greed, will cost my crown, and like a hungry eagle tear and feast on the flesh of me and of my son!

"The loss of those three lords — the Earl of Westmoreland, the Earl of Northumberland, and Lord Clifford — torments my heart. I'll write to them very courteously.

"Come, kinsman Exeter, you shall be the messenger."

The Duke of Exeter said, "And I, I hope, shall reconcile them all to you."

Richard and Edward, who were two of the Duke of York's sons, and the Marquess of Montague talked together in the Duke of York's castle: Sandal Castle, located near Wakefield in West Yorkshire.

They were discussing who should talk to the Duke of York.

Richard said to Edward, "Brother, although I am the youngest, allow me to be the one to speak to our father."

"No, I can better play the orator," Edward said.

The Marquess of Montague said, "But I have strong and forceful arguments that I can make to him."

The Duke of York entered the room and said, "Why, what's going on now, sons and brother! Engaging in a disagreement? What is your quarrel? How did it first begin?"

"No quarrel, but a slight contention," Edward said.

The contention was the disagreement among the three as well as the contention for the crown of the King of England.

"A contention about what?" the Duke of York asked.

"About that which concerns your grace and us," Richard said. "The crown of England, father, which is yours."

"Mine, son?" the Duke of York said. "It's not mine until King Henry VI is dead."

"Your right to the crown does not depend on King Henry VI's life or death," Richard said.

Edward said, "Now you are heir to the crown, so therefore enjoy the crown now. By giving the House of Lancaster the opportunity to catch its breath and recover, it will outrun you, father, in the end."

"I took an oath that King Henry VI should quietly reign until his death," the Duke of York said.

Edward said, "But for a Kingdom any oath may be broken. I would break a thousand oaths to reign one year."

A proverb stated, "For a Kingdom any law may be broken."

"No," Richard said. "God forbid that your grace should be forsworn."

"I shall be forsworn, if I claim the crown by open war," the Duke of York said.

"I'll prove that you will not be forsworn, if you'll hear what I have to say," Richard said.

"You cannot, son," the Duke of York said. "It is impossible."

Richard said, "An oath is of no importance, if it was not made before a true and lawful magistrate who has authority over the man who swears the oath.

"Henry VI had no authority because he usurped his Kingdom. So then, seeing that it was Henry VI who made you swear an oath, your oath, my lord, is worthless and groundless.

"Therefore, to arms! Fight for your crown! And, father, think how sweet a thing it is to wear a crown. Within the crown's circumference is the classical paradise known as Elysium, and within the crown's circumference is all that poets depict of bliss and joy.

"Why do we linger like this? I cannot rest until the white rose that I am wearing is dyed in the lukewarm blood of Henry VI's heart."

The Duke of York said, "Richard, enough; I will be King, or die."

"Marquess of Montague, my brother, you shall go to London immediately and encourage Warwick to do his part in this enterprise.

"You, Richard, shall go to the Duke of Norfolk, and tell him secretly and privately what we intend to do.

"You, Edward, shall go to my Lord Cobham, with whom the Kentishmen will willingly rise up in rebellion against Henry VI. In them I trust, for they are soldiers who are intelligent, courteous, generous, and full of spirit.

"While you are thus employed, what is left to be done other than for me to seek an opportunity to rise without Henry VI and any of the House of Lancaster being aware of my intention?"

A messenger ran into the room.

The Duke of York said, "But wait."

He said to the messenger, "What is the news? Why have you come in such haste?"

The messenger replied, "The Queen with all the northern Earls and lords intends to besiege you here in your castle. She is close by with twenty thousand men; therefore, fortify your stronghold, my lord."

"Yes, with my sword," the Duke of York said. "What! Do you think that we fear them?

"Edward and Richard, you shall stay with me.

"My brother Montague shall hurry to London. Let noble Warwick, Cobham, and the rest, whom we have left as Protectors of the King, strengthen themselves with powerful political sagacity and not trust simple, foolish Henry or his oaths."

"Brother, I go now," the Marquess of Montague said. "I'll win the Londoners over to your side — don't fear that I won't! And thus most humbly I take my leave."

He exited.

Sir John Mortimer and Sir Hugh Mortimer entered the room. They were uncles of the Duke of York.

The Duke of York said, "Sir John and Sir Hugh Mortimer, my uncles, you have come to Sandal Castle in a happy hour. It is good that you are here because the army of Queen Margaret intends to besiege us."

"She shall not need to," Sir John Mortimer said. "We'll meet her in the battlefield."

"What, with five thousand men?" the Duke of York asked.

"Yes, with five hundred, father, if need be," Richard said. "A woman is the General; what should we fear?"

Marching drums sounded in the distance.

"I hear their drums," Edward said. "Let's set our men in order, and issue forth and offer them battle at once."

"Five men to twenty!" the Duke of York said. "Although the odds are great, I don't doubt, uncle, that we will be victorious. Many battles have I won in France, when the enemy has outnumbered my soldiers ten to one. Why should I not now have the same success and victory that I have enjoyed before now?"

— 1.3 —

On 30 December 1460, the Battle of Wakefield was taking place. One of the Duke of York's sons, young Rutland, and his tutor were in danger.

Rutland asked, "Where shall I flee to escape their hands?"

Lord Clifford and some soldiers arrived.

Seeing them, Rutland said, "Tutor, look where bloodthirsty Clifford comes!"

Lord Clifford said to the tutor, who, like many teachers of the time, was also a religious man and therefore knew Latin, "Chaplain, away! Your priesthood saves your life. As for this accursed Duke of York's brat, this brat whose father slew my father, he shall die."

The tutor replied, "And I, my lord, will bear him company."

Lord Clifford ordered, "Soldiers, take him away!"

The tutor pleaded, "Clifford, don't murder this innocent child, lest you be hated both by God and by men!"

The soldiers dragged away the tutor.

Rutland shut his eyes in fear.

Lord Clifford said, "What is this! Is he dead already? Or is it fear that makes him close his eyes? I'll open them."

Rutland opened his eyes and said, "So looks the confined, ravenous lion over the wretch that trembles under his devouring paws, and so the lion walks, exulting over his prey, and so the lion comes, to rend his limbs asunder.

"Ah, noble Clifford, kill me with your sword, and not with such a cruel threatening look. Sweet Clifford, hear me speak before I die. I am too mean a subject for your wrath: Be revenged on men, and let me live."

"You speak in vain, poor boy," Clifford said. "My father's blood has stopped the passage where your words should enter."

"Then let my father's blood open it again," Rutland pleaded. "He is a man, and so, Clifford, fight him."

"If I had all your male relatives here, their lives and yours would not be sufficient revenge for me. No, if I dug up your forefathers' graves and hung their rotten coffins up in chains, it would not slake my anger, nor would it ease my heart. The sight of any of the House of York is like a Fury — an ancient avenging goddess — to torment my soul, and until I root out York's accursed family and leave not one alive, I live in Hell. Therefore —"

He lifted his sword.

Rutland pleaded, "Oh, let me pray before I take my death! To you I pray: Sweet Clifford, pity me!"

He knelt.

"I will give you such pity as my rapier's point affords," Lord Clifford said.

"I never did you harm," Rutland said. "Why will you slay me?"

"Your father has done me harm," Lord Clifford replied.

"But it was before I was born," Rutland said. "You have one son; for his sake pity me, lest in revenge for your murdering me, since God is just, your son will be as miserably slain as I am. Let me live in prison for all my days, and when I give you a reason to be offended, then let me die, for now you have no cause to kill me."

"No cause!" Lord Clifford said. "Your father slew my father; therefore, die."

Lord Clifford stabbed the boy.

Dying, Rutland said, "*Di faciant laudis summa sit ista tuae*!"

This is Latin for "May the gods grant that this be your crowning praise!"

In other words, "May you be most remembered for murdering a boy!"

"Plantagenet! I am coming for you, Plantagenet!" Lord Clifford said, referring to the Duke of York. "And this your son's blood that cleaves to my blade shall rust upon my weapon until your blood, congealed with this blood of your son, makes me wipe off both."

In another part of the battlefield, the Duke of York mourned the loss of the battle.

He said to himself, "The army of Queen Margaret has won the battle and controls the battlefield. Both of my uncles the Mortimers were slain as they rescued me, and all my followers turn their back to the fierce foe and flee, like ships before the wind or lambs pursued by hunger-emaciated wolves.

"God knows what has happened to my sons, but this I know: They have behaved like men born to be renowned either because of their life or because of their death. Three times Richard made a lane of dead enemy soldiers as he cut a path to me, and three times he cried, 'Courage, father! Fight it out!' And just as often Edward came to my side, with a red sword, painted to the hilt with the blood of those enemies who had encountered him.

"And when our hardiest warriors retreated, Richard cried, 'Charge! And give no foot of ground!' And he cried, 'A crown, or else a glorious tomb! A scepter, or an earthly sepulcher!'

"With this, we charged again, but alas! We retreated again, as I have seen a swan with useless labor swim against the tide and expend her strength against overwhelming waves."

He heard a call to arms.

He said, "Listen! The fatal followers pursue my soldiers and me, and I am faint and cannot flee from their fury. Even if I were strong, I would not shun their fury. The grains of sand in the hourglass that make up my life are so few in number that they can be counted. Here I must stay, and here my life must end."

Queen Margaret, Lord Clifford, the Earl of Northumberland, Prince Edward, and some soldiers arrived.

The Duke of York said, "Come, bloodthirsty Clifford. Come, cruel Northumberland, I dare your quenchless fury to more rage. I am your target, and I await your shot."

The Earl of Northumberland said to the Duke of York, "Yield to our mercy, proud Plantagenet."

"Yes," Lord Clifford said, "yield to such mercy as the Duke of York's ruthless arm, with downright payment — directed straight down, in the form of a sword

— showed to my father. Now Phaëthon has tumbled from his car, and made an evening at the noontide prick — the mark on the Sun-dial that indicates noon."

Phaëthon was the son of Apollo the Sun-god. He asked Apollo to prove that he was his father by giving him a gift. Apollo swore an inviolable oath to give him any gift he asked for, and Phaëthon asked to be allowed to drive the Sun-chariot across the sky. Having sworn an inviolable oath, Apollo had no choice but to allow him to do it. Phaëthon was unable to control the immortal horses that pulled the Sun-chariot, and at times the Sun-chariot came too close to the Earth, making everything too hot, and at other times it went too far away from the Earth, causing darkness. The King of the gods, Jupiter, saved the Earth by hurling a thunderbolt at Phaëthon, killing him and causing him to fall out of the Sun-chariot. Apollo took his place in the Sun-chariot and restored order.

The Duke of York said, "My ashes, as happens with the Phoenix, may bring forth a bird that will get revenge on you all."

The Phoenix was a mythical bird of Arabia that lived for 500 years and then died in a burst of fire but was regenerated from its ashes. In fact, the Duke of York's sons Edward and Richard would get revenge for their father's death.

The Duke of York continued, "And in that hope I throw my eyes — I look — to Heaven, scorning whatever you can afflict me with.

"Why don't you attack me? What! There are multitudes of you, and you are afraid to attack me?"

Lord Clifford said, "So cowards fight when they can flee no further. So doves peck the falcon's piercing talons. So desperate thieves, completely despairing of saving their lives, vehemently speak invectives against the officers who will give them capital punishment."

A proverb stated, "Despair makes cowards courageous."

The Duke of York said, "Clifford, think once again, and in your thoughts review my past, and then see if you can avoid blushing and biting your tongue, which slanders me with cowardice as you view this face, whose frown has made you lose heart and flee before this time!"

Lord Clifford replied, "I will not exchange words with you word for word, but I will exchange blows with you, giving you four blows for each blow you give me."

He made a move toward the Duke of York, but Queen Margaret cried, "Wait, valiant Clifford! For a thousand reasons, I want to prolong for a while this traitor's life."

Lord Clifford was still angry and kept moving toward the Duke of York, and Queen Margaret said, "Wrath makes him deaf."

Others restrained Lord Clifford, and Queen Margaret said, "Speak, Earl of Northumberland."

He said, "Stop, Clifford! Don't honor him so much by pricking your finger, although it would wound his heart. What valor would one get, when a cur bares its teeth, if one were to thrust his hand between the cur's teeth, when he might kick him away with his foot? War allows one to take all advantages, and ten against one is no impeachment of valor. In times of war, one ought not to fight an enemy one against one when enough soldiers are available to fight an enemy ten against one."

They fought the Duke of York, who struggled against them but was subdued.

Clifford said, "Yes, yes, like this the woodcock strives with the trap."

A woodcock is a proverbially stupid and easily caught bird.

The Earl of Northumberland said, "Like this the rabbit struggles in the net."

The Duke of York said, "Like this thieves gloat upon their conquered booty. Like this true men yield, when so outnumbered by robbers."

The Earl of Northumberland said to Queen Margaret, "What would your grace have done to him now?"

"You brave warriors, Clifford and Northumberland, come, make him stand upon this molehill here," Queen Margaret replied. "He reached out for mountains with outstretched arms, yet with his hand took as his own only their shadow."

She said to the Duke of York, "Was it you who would be England's King? Was it you who rioted in our Parliament and made a sermon about your high descent? Where is your mess of sons — your four sons — to back you now? Where are the wanton Edward, and the vigorous George? And where's that valiant hunchback monster, your boy Dicky, who with his grumbling voice was accustomed to cheer his dad in mutinies?

"And, along with the rest, where is your darling Rutland? Look, York: I stained this handkerchief with the blood that valiant Clifford with his rapier's point made flow from the bosom of the boy. And if your eyes can water for his death, I give you this handkerchief to dry your cheeks with.

"Alas, poor York! Except that I so deadly hate you, I would lament your miserable state. I ask you to grieve so you can make me merry, York.

"Has your fiery heart so parched your entrails that not a tear can fall for Rutland's death? Why are you patient, man? You should be mad, and I, to make you mad, mock you. Stamp your feet, rave, and fret so that I may sing and dance.

"You want to be paid, I see, to entertain me. York cannot speak, unless he wears a crown. Here's a crown for York!

"Lords, bow low to him. Restrain his hands while I set the crown on his head."

She placed a paper crown on the Duke of York's head.

She continued, "Yes, by the Virgin Mary, sir, now he looks like a King! Yes, this is the man who took King Henry VI's throne, and this is the man who was his adopted heir.

"But how is it that great Plantagenet has been crowned so soon, and has broken his solemn oath? As I remember, you should not be King until our King Henry VI has shaken hands with Death.

"And will you encircle your head with Henry's glory, and rob his temples of the diadem, now, during his life, against your holy oath?

"Oh, it is a crime too, too unpardonable!

"Off with the crown, and with the crown take off his head. While we breathe, let's take time to do him dead. While we're alive, let's kill him."

"That is my job, for my father's sake," Lord Clifford said.

"No, wait," Queen Margaret said. "Let's hear the prayers he makes."

The Duke of York said, "She-wolf of France, but worse than the wolves of France. Your tongue is more poisonous than the adder's tooth!

"How ill-beseeming is it for one of your sex to triumph, like an Amazonian warrior-woman whore, upon the woes of men whom Lady Fortune has made captives!

"Except that your face, mask-like and unchanging, has been made impudent with the habitual practice of evil deeds, I would attempt, proud Queen, to make you blush.

"To tell you where you came from and who are your parents would be shame enough to shame you, if you were not shameless.

"Your father bears the title of King of Naples, Sicily, and Jerusalem, yet he is not as wealthy as an English farmer.

"Has that poor monarch taught you to be insolent? Showing insolence is not necessary, nor does it help you, proud Queen, unless this adage must be verified: Beggars, once mounted, run their horse to death.

"Beauty often makes women proud, but God knows that your share of beauty is small.

"Virtue makes women most admired, but your lack of virtue makes people look at you with wonder.

"Self-government — self-control — makes women seem divine, but your lack of self-control makes you abominable.

"You are as opposite to every good as the Antipodes — the people who live on the other side of the world — are to us, or as the south is to the Septentrion."

The Septentrion is the north. The name derives from the Latin *septentriōnēs*, which means "seven plowing oxen." This refers to the seven stars that make up the asterism known as the Plow, also referred to as the Big Dipper, which is part of the constellation *Ursa Major*, or Great Bear.

The Duke of York continued, "Oh, tiger's heart wrapped in a woman's hide! How could you drain the life-blood of the child so you could bid the father wipe his eyes with a handkerchief stained with that blood, and yet be seen to bear a woman's face?

"Women are soft, mild, pitiful, and flexible, but you are stern, obdurate, flinty, rough, and remorseless.

"You want me to rage? Why, now you have your wish. You want me to weep? Why, now you have what you want.

"For raging wind blows up incessant showers, and when the rage allays, the rain begins. These tears I shed are my sweet Rutland's obsequies and funeral rites, and every drop cries out for vengeance for his death, against you, cruel Clifford, and you, false Frenchwoman."

The Earl of Northumberland thought, *Curse me, but his passion moves me so that I can hardly keep my eyes from shedding tears.*

The Duke of York continued speaking to Queen Margaret, "The hungry cannibals would not have touched Rutland's face, would not have stained this handkerchief with his blood, but you are more inhuman, more inexorable, oh, ten times more, than the tigers of Hyrcania.

"See, ruthless Queen, a hapless father's tears. You dipped this handkerchief in the blood of my sweet boy, and I wash the blood away with my tears.

"Keep the handkerchief and go boast about this; if you tell the sorrowful story correctly, I swear upon my soul that the hearers will shed tears. Yes, even my enemies will shed fast-falling tears, and they will say, 'Alas, it was a piteous deed!'"

He shook the paper crown from his head and said, "There, Queen Margaret, take the crown, and, with the crown, take my curse. And in your need may such comfort come to you as I reap now at your too cruel hand!

"Hard-hearted Clifford, take me from the world. My soul will go to Heaven, and my blood is upon your heads!"

His eyes watering, the Earl of Northumberland thought, *Had he been the executioner of all my kinfolk, I would not for my life be able to avoid weeping with him when I see how inwardly sorrow grips his soul.*

Queen Margaret said to him, "What, ready to weep, my Lord Northumberland? Only think upon the wrong he did us all, and that will quickly dry your melting tears."

Lord Clifford said as he stabbed the Duke of York, "Here's for my oath, and here's for my father's death."

Queen Margaret said as she stabbed the Duke of York, "And here's to redress the injuries of our gentle-hearted King."

"Open your gate of mercy, gracious God!" the Duke of York cried. "My soul flies through these wounds to seek out You."

He died.

Queen Margaret said, "Cut off his head, and set it on the town of York's gates, so that the Duke of York may look out over the town of York."

CHAPTER 2

— 2.1 —

Edward and Richard, two of the Duke of York's three surviving sons (the other surviving son was George, who was soon to be the Duke of Clarence), talked together on a plain near Mortimer's Cross in Herefordshire, not far from the border with Wales. Also present were some of their soldiers.

Edward said, "I wonder how our Princely father escaped, or whether he escaped away from Clifford's and Northumberland's pursuit. If he had been captured, we should have heard the news. If he had been slain, we should have heard the news. Or if he had escaped, I think we should have heard the happy tidings of his good escape.

"How are you, my brother? Why are you so sad?"

Richard replied, "I cannot feel joy until I know what has become of our very valiant father. I saw him in the battle ranging about, and I watched how he singled Clifford out as if he were hunting him. I thought our father bore himself in the thickest troop of enemy soldiers as a lion does in a herd of cattle, or as a dog-surrounded bear, having bitten a few dogs and made them cry, makes the remaining dogs stand at a distance and bark at him. So our father fared with his enemies, and so his enemies fled my warlike father.

"I think that it is prize enough to be his son. See how the morning opens her golden gates, and takes her farewell of the glorious Sun! Aurora, goddess of dawn, says farewell to the Sun! How well the Sun resembles the prime of youth, dressed like a young man prancing to his love!"

"Are my eyes dazzled, or do I see three Suns?" Edward asked.

Richard said, "Three glorious Suns, each one a perfect Sun. They are not separated by the wind-driven clouds, but severed in a pale, clear-shining sky."

The three Suns began to join together.

Richard continued, "Look, look! They join, embrace, and seem to kiss, as if they vowed some inviolable alliance. Now are they but one lamp, one light, one Sun. In this, Heaven prefigures some event. This is an omen."

The Sun was the emblem — the distinctive badge — of the House of York.

Edward said, "It is wondrously strange; the like was never heard of so far. I think it incites us, brother, to go to the battlefield, so that we, the sons of brave Plantagenet, Duke of York, each one already blazing by our merited deserts, should notwithstanding join our lights together and shine over the earth as this Sun shines over the world. Whatever it bodes, henceforward I will bear three fair-shining Suns as a heraldic device on my shield."

Richard said, "No, bear three daughters. If you don't mind my saying so, I say that you love the breeder better than the male. You love women."

A messenger arrived, and Richard asked, "Who are you, whose sorrowful looks foretell some dreadful story hanging on your tongue?"

The messenger replied, "I am one who was a woeful looker-on when the noble Duke of York, your Princely father and my loving lord, was slain!"

Edward said, "Oh, speak no more, for I have heard too much."

Richard said, "Say how he died, for I will hear it all."

The messenger said, "Many foes surrounded him, and he stood against them, as the hope of Troy — Hector — stood against the Greeks who would have entered Troy. But even Hercules himself must yield to odds, and many strokes, although made with a little axe, will hew down and fell the hardest-timbered oak.

"By many hands your father was subdued, but he was slaughtered only by the angry arms of unrelenting Clifford and Queen Margaret, who crowned the gracious Duke in great scorn, laughed in his face, and when with grief he wept, the ruthless Queen gave him to dry his cheeks a handkerchief steeped in the harmless blood of sweet young Rutland, who was slain by violent Clifford.

"And after many scorns and many foul taunts, they took off his head, and on the gates of the town of York they set the head, and there it remains, the saddest spectacle that I ever viewed."

Edward said, "Sweet Duke of York, our prop to lean upon, now that you are gone, we have no staff, no support.

"Oh, Clifford, savage Clifford! You have slain a man who for his chivalry was the flower of Europe, and you have vanquished him by treachery, for he would have vanquished you if you had fought him hand to hand.

"Now my soul's palace has become a prison. I wish that my soul would break from my body, so that this body of mine might be enclosed in the ground and rest! For never henceforth shall I enjoy life again, never, oh, never shall I see enjoyment any more!"

Richard said, "I cannot weep, for all my body's moisture scarcely serves to quench my heart that burns like a furnace. Nor can my tongue unload my heart's great burden, for that same wind that I should speak with is kindling coals that fire all my breast, and burns me up with flames that my tears would quench.

"To weep is to make less the depth of grief. Tears then are for babes; blows and revenge are what I want.

"Richard, Duke of York, I bear your name; I am also a Richard. I'll avenge your death, or die renowned by attempting it."

Edward said, "His name that valiant Duke has left with you. His Dukedom and his chair — his ducal seat — he left with me."

As the oldest son, Edward was now the new Duke of York and held the Dukedom.

Richard said, "If you are that Princely eagle's fledgling, show your descent by gazing at the Sun. Say 'For ducal seat and Dukedom' and 'For throne and Kingdom.' Either those things are yours, or else you are not our father's son."

This society believed that the eagle was the King of the birds, and as such was able to look directly at the Sun.

A drum sounded a march, and the Earl of Warwick, the Marquess of Montague, and some soldiers arrived.

"How are you, fair lords?" the Earl of Warwick asked. "How do you fare? What is the news from abroad?"

"Great Lord of Warwick," Richard said, "if we would recount our baleful news, and at each word's deliverance stab daggers in our flesh until all were told, the words would add more anguish than the wounds.

"Oh, valiant lord, the Duke of York has been slain!"

"Oh, Warwick, Warwick!" Edward said, "that Plantagenet, who held you as dearly as his soul's redemption, has been killed by the stern Lord Clifford."

"Ten days ago I drowned this news with my tears," the Earl of Warwick replied, "and now, to add even more to your woes, I have come to tell you things since then befallen.

"After the bloody fray we fought at Wakefield, where your brave father breathed his last gasp, tidings, as swiftly as the messengers could travel, were brought to me of your loss and his departure from this life.

"I, who was then in London as keeper of King Henry VI, mustered my soldiers, gathered flocks of friends, and very well armed and equipped, so I thought, marched toward Saint Albans to intercept Queen Margaret, and I brought the King along as I thought his presence might be useful.

"I did all this because my scouts informed me that Queen Margaret was coming with a full intention to rescind our recent decree in Parliament concerning King Henry VI's oath and your succession as King after his death.

"To make it a short tale, we met on 17 February 1461 and at Saint Albans fought the Second Battle of St. Albans.

"Our armies joined in battle, and both sides fiercely fought, but whether it was the coldness and lack of passion of the King, who looked very gently on his warlike Queen, that robbed my soldiers of their inflamed spirit, or whether it was the report of the Queen's success, or whether it was the more than common fear of the harshness of Clifford, who thunders blood and death to his captives, I cannot judge, but to conclude with the truth, the enemies' weapons struck as if they were lightning as they came and went. Our soldiers' weapons struck like the night owl's lazy flight, or like an idle thresher with a flail for reaping grain. Our soldiers' weapons fell gently down, as if they were striking their friends.

"I revived them by telling them of the justice of our cause, and with the promise of high pay and great rewards, but all in vain. They had no heart to fight, and we had no hope in them to win the day.

"And so we fled. The King fled to the Queen. Your brother Lord George, as well as the Duke of Norfolk and I, fled in haste, as quickly as we could, to come to join with you, for we heard you were here in the marches — the Welsh borders — gathering another army with which to fight again."

"Where is the Duke of Norfolk, noble Warwick?" Edward asked. "And when did George come from Burgundy to England?"

"The Duke of Norfolk is some six miles away with the soldiers," the Earl of Warwick said. "And as for your brother, your kind aunt, the Duchess of Burgundy, recently sent him here with the aid of soldiers to this war because you need reinforcements."

"The odds must have been against our side, most likely, when valiant Warwick fled," Richard said. "Often have I heard his praises in pursuit, but never until now have I heard the scandalous imputations of his retiring from the battle."

"And you do not now hear of any scandal affecting me, Richard," the Earl of Warwick said, "for you shall learn that this strong right hand of mine can pluck the diadem from fainthearted Henry VI's head, and wring the awe-inspiring scepter from his fist, even if he were as famous and as bold in war as he is famed for mildness, peace, and prayer."

"I know it well, Lord Warwick," Richard said. "Don't blame me. It is the love I bear your glories that makes me speak. But in this troublous time what's to be done?

"Shall we throw away our coats of steel, and wrap our bodies in black mourning gowns, and count our Ave-Maries with our beads?

"Or shall we on the helmets of our foes count with our blows our devotion with revengeful weapons?

"If you vote for the last alternative, say yes, and let's go to it, lords."

The Earl of Warwick replied, "Why, that is the reason that I, Warwick, came to seek you. And for that same reason my brother Montague came to seek you.

"Listen to me, lords. The proud insulting Queen Margaret, with Clifford and the haughty Northumberland, and many more proud birds of the same feather, have molded the easily pliable and persuadable King like wax.

"Previously, he swore consent to your succession and he recorded his oath in the Parliament, but now to London all that crew have gone to annul both his oath and to do in addition whatever may make trouble against the House of Lancaster.

"Their army, I think, is thirty thousand strong. Now, if the help of the Duke of Norfolk and myself, with all the friends that you, Edward, who are the brave Earl of March, can procure among the friendly Welshmen, will at least amount to twenty-five thousand, why, *Via*!"

"*Via*!" is Italian for "Forward!"

The Earl of Warwick continued, "To London we will march at full speed, and once again we will bestride our foaming steeds, and once again cry, 'Charge upon our foes!' But never will we once again turn our backs and flee."

Richard said, "Yes, now I think I hear great Warwick speak. May that man never live to see a sunshiny day who cries 'Retreat,' if Warwick orders him to stay and fight."

"Lord Warwick, I will lean on your shoulder," Edward said, "and when you fail — may God forbid the hour! — then Edward must fall, which peril may Heaven forbid!"

The Earl of Warwick said, "No longer Earl of March, you are the Duke of York. The next step up is England's royal throne, for you shall be proclaimed King of England in every borough as we pass along, and that man who does not throw his cap up in the air for joy shall for that crime make forfeit of his head.

"King Edward IV, valiant Richard, Marquess of Montague, let's stay no longer, dreaming of renown, but let the trumpets sound, and go about achieving our task."

Richard addressed an absent enemy, "Lord Clifford, even if your heart were as hard as steel, as you have shown it to be flinty by your deeds, I am coming to you to pierce it, or to give you mine."

Edward said, "Then strike up drums. God and Saint George for us!"

Saint George is the patron saint of England.

A messenger arrived.

The Earl of Warwick asked, "What is it? What is the news?"

The messenger replied, "The Duke of Norfolk sends you word by me that Queen Margaret is coming with a powerful army. He requests your company for speedy counsel."

The Earl of Warwick said, "Why, then everything is working out well. Brave warriors, let's go."

— 2.2 —

King Henry VI, Queen Margaret, Prince Edward, Lord Clifford, and the Earl of Northumberland stood in front of the town of York. With them were soldiers, including a drummer and a trumpeter.

Queen Margaret said to her husband, King Henry VI, "Welcome, my lord, to this brave town of York. Yonder is the head of that archenemy, the Duke of York, who sought to have your crown encircle his head. Doesn't the object cheer your heart, my lord?"

"Yes," King Henry VI said, "as much as the rocks cheer those who fear their ship will wreck on them. To see this sight irks my very soul. Withhold revenge, dear God! It is not my fault, for I have not deliberately infringed my vow."

King Henry VI was worried that he had violated his oath. He had sworn to allow the Duke of York and the Duke's heirs to have the crown after he died, but Queen Margaret and Lord Clifford had been waging war to have the oath annulled.

Lord Clifford said, "My gracious liege, this excessive mildness and gentleness and harmful pity must be laid aside. To whom do lions cast their gentle looks? Not to the beast that would usurp their den. Whose hand does the wild forest bear lick? Not his who carries away her young before her face. Who escapes the lurking serpent's deadly sting? Not he who sets his foot upon her back. The smallest snake will attack after being trodden on, and doves will peck to safeguard their brood.

"The ambitious York aimed at your crown, and you smile while he knits his angry brows. He, who was only a Duke, wanted his son to be a King, and he wanted to elevate in rank his offspring, like a loving sire.

"You, who are a King, blest with an excellent son, gave your consent to disinherit him, which argued that you are a very unloving father.

"Creatures that are incapable of reason feed their young, and although man's face is frightening to their eyes, yet who has not seen them protect their tender ones with those wings that sometimes they have used in fearful flight and make war against that person who climbed to their nest, and offer their own lives in their young's defense?

"For shame, my liege, make them your precedent! Wouldn't it be a pity that this excellent boy should lose his birthright by his father's fault, and long hereafter say to his child, 'What my great-grandfather and grandfather got, my heedless father foolishly gave away'?"

The great-grandfather and grandfather of Edward, Prince of Wales, were King Henry IV, who took the crown from King Richard II, and King Henry V, who became a national hero because of his victories in France.

Lord Clifford continued, "Ah, what a shame that would be! Look on the boy, and let his manly face, which promises a successful fortune, steel your melting heart to hold your own and leave your own with him. Look at your son and resolve to be King and let him be King after you."

King Henry VI replied, "Very well has Clifford played the orator, making arguments of mighty force. But, Clifford, tell me, did you never hear that things ill gotten always have bad outcomes? And were things always happy for that son whose father went to Hell because of his hoarding? I'll leave behind my virtuous deeds for my son, and I wish that my father had left me no more than that! For all the rest is held at such a rate as brings a thousand-fold more care to keep than possession brings jot of pleasure."

He then said to the Duke of York's decapitated head, "Ah, kinsman York! I wish your best friends knew how much it grieves me that your head is here!"

Queen Margaret said to him, "My lord, cheer up your spirits. Our foes are near, and this soft courage makes your followers fainthearted. You promised knighthood to our early-maturing son. Unsheathe your sword, and dub him a knight immediately.

"Edward, Prince of Wales, kneel down."

Prince Edward knelt, and King Henry VI tapped his shoulders with a sword and then said, "Edward Plantagenet, arise a knight, and learn this lesson: Draw your sword in justice."

The House of Lancaster and the House of York were both descended from King Edward III, whose family name was Plantagenet.

Prince Edward said, "My gracious father, by your Kingly leave, I'll draw my sword as heir apparent to the crown, and in that cause use it to the death."

Lord Clifford said, "Why, that is spoken like a promising Prince."

A messenger arrived and said, "Royal commanders, be in readiness, for with a band of thirty thousand men comes Warwick, with the support of Edward, the new Duke of York, and in the towns, as they march along, people proclaim him King, and many run to him. Arrange your troops in fighting position, for the enemy soldiers are near at hand."

Lord Clifford said to King Henry VI, "I wish that your highness would depart from the battlefield. The Queen has best success when you are absent."

Queen Margaret said, "Yes, my good lord, depart and leave us to our fortune."

King Henry VI replied, "Why, that's my fortune, too; therefore, I'll stay."

The Earl of Northumberland said, "If you stay, stay with resolution then to fight."

"My royal father," Prince Edward said, "cheer these noble lords and hearten those who fight in your defense. Unsheathe your sword, good father; cry 'Saint George!'"

A marching drum sounded, and the three surviving sons of the Duke of York — Edward, George, and Richard — arrived. With them were the Earl of Warwick, the Duke of Norfolk, the Marquess of Montague, and some soldiers. They had come for a parley.

Edward said, "Now, perjured Henry, will you kneel for grace and set your diadem upon my head, or will you endure the deadly fortune of the battlefield?"

Queen Margaret said, "Go and berate your minions, proud insulting boy! Is it becoming for you to speak so boldly before your sovereign and lawful King?"

"I am his King, and he should bow his knee to me," Edward said. "I was adopted heir by his consent. Since that time, his oath has been broken, for as I hear, you, Margaret, who are King although he wears the crown, have caused him by a new act of Parliament to blot me out of the succession and put his own son in."

"And with good reason, too," Lord Clifford said. "Who should succeed the father but the son?"

Richard said, "Are you there, butcher? Oh, I cannot speak!"

Richard was calling Lord Clifford a butcher because he had killed young Rutland.

Lord Clifford replied, "Yes, crookback, here I stand to answer you or any man who is the proudest of your gang."

"It was you who killed young Rutland, wasn't it?" Richard asked.

"Yes, and the old Duke of York, and I am not yet satisfied," Lord Clifford replied.

"For God's sake, lords, give the signal to begin the battle," Richard said.

"What do you say, Henry?" the Earl of Warwick asked. "Will you yield the crown?"

Queen Margaret said, "Why, what is this, long-tongued, chattering Warwick! Do you dare to speak? When you and I last met at Saint Albans, your legs did better service for you than your hands."

"Then it was my turn to flee, and now it is yours," the Earl of Warwick said.

"You said that before," Lord Clifford said, "and yet you fled."

"It was not your valor, Clifford, that drove me away," the Earl of Warwick said.

"No," the Earl of Northumberland said, "nor was it your manhood that dared to make you stay."

"Northumberland, I regard you with great esteem," Richard said.

He added, "Break off the parley; for I can scarcely refrain from putting into action the passions of my big-swollen heart against Clifford, that cruel child-killer."

"I slew your father," Lord Clifford said. "Do you call him a child?"

Richard ignored that comment, but he said, "Like a dastardly and treacherous coward, you killed our young brother Rutland, but before sunset I'll make you curse the deed."

"Have done with words, my lords, and hear me speak," King Henry VI said.

"Defy them then, or else close your lips," Queen Margaret said to him.

"Please, put no limits on my tongue. I am a King, and I have the privilege of speaking," Henry VI said.

"My liege," Lord Clifford said, "the wound that bred this meeting here cannot be cured by words; therefore, be still and quiet."

"Then, executioner, unsheathe your sword," Richard said. "By Him Who made us all, I am resolved that Clifford's manhood lies upon his tongue. His tongue is more manly than his sword."

"Tell me, Henry, shall I have my rights, or not?" Edward asked King Henry VI. "A thousand men have broken their fasts today who shall never eat the evening meal unless you yield the crown to me."

The Earl of Warwick said to King Henry VI, "If you deny Edward the crown, the blood of the soldiers who will die is upon your head because Edward, the new Duke of York, puts his armor on for a just cause."

Prince Edward said, "If that is right which Warwick says is right, then there is no wrong, but everything is right."

Richard said to Prince Edward, "Whichever man begot you, there your mother stands, for I know well that you have your mother's tongue."

Queen Margaret said to Richard, "But you are like neither your sire nor your dam."

This was an insult because "dam" is a word used for an animal's mother.

She continued, "But you are like a foul misshapen deformed individual, marked by the destinies as a person to be avoided just like venomous toads or lizards' dreadful stings."

Richard replied, "You are iron of Naples hidden with a covering of English gilt, and your father bears the title of a King — as if a gutter should be called the sea. Aren't you ashamed, knowing from whom you are descended, to let your tongue reveal your basely born heart?"

Richard was pointing out that Margaret had married above her social rank. Her father was a titular King with little money, and yet she had married the King of England.

Edward, Duke of York, said, "A wisp of straw would be worth a thousand crowns if it were possible to make this shameless whore know herself.

"Helen of Greece was fairer far than you, although your husband may be Menelaus, and never was Agamemnon's brother wronged by that false woman, as this King has been wronged by you."

Edward, Duke of York, thought little of Helen of Greece, who became Helen of Troy. He believed that she had cuckolded Menelaus, her lawful husband, by running away with the Trojan Prince Paris.

Edward, Duke of York, continued, "Henry VI's father reveled in the heart of France, and tamed the King of France, and made the French King's oldest son — the Dauphin — stoop.

"And if Henry VI had married according to his rank and position, he might have kept that glory of being King of England to this day. But when he took a beggar to his bed, and graced your poor father by marrying you, even then that sunshine brewed a shower for him — a shower that washed away the victories that his father — Henry V — had won in France.

"That shower also heaped sedition on his crown at home. For what has broached this tumult but your pride? Had you been meek, our title to the crown would have continued to sleep because we, in pity of the gentle King Henry VI, would have not asserted our claim to the crown until another age."

George said, "But when we saw our sunshine made your spring, and we saw that your summer bred us no growth, we set the axe to your usurping root, and although the edge of the axe has to some extent hit ourselves, yet you should know that since we have begun to strike, we'll never stop until we have hewn you down, or bathed and fertilized your growth with our heated blood."

Duke Edward of York said, "And with that resolution, I defy you. I am not willing any longer to engage in talk, since you will not allow the gentle King to speak.

"Let the trumpets sound! Let our bloodthirsty battle flags wave! And let us get either victory, or else a grave."

"Stay, Edward," Queen Margaret said.

"No, wrangling woman, we'll no longer stay," Duke Edward of York said. "These angry words we have exchanged will cost ten thousand lives this day."

The Battle of Towton was taking place on 29 March 1461 on a battlefield near Leeds in Yorkshire. An exhausted Earl of Warwick stood alone.

The Earl of Warwick said, "Exhausted with toil, as runners with a race, I lay me down a little while to rest, for strokes received, and many blows repaid, have robbed my strongly knit muscles of their strength, and come what may I must rest awhile."

Duke Edward of York arrived, running, and said, "Smile, gentle, noble Heaven! Or strike, ungentle, ignoble death! For this world frowns, and Edward's sun is clouded."

"What is it, my lord!" the Earl of Warwick asked. "What has happened? What hope of good fortune do we have?"

George arrived and said, "Our fortune is loss, and our hope is only sad despair. Our ranks are broken, and ruin follows us. What counsel can you give? Whither shall we flee?"

"Fight is useless," Edward said. "They follow us with wings, and we are weak and cannot avoid pursuit."

Richard arrived and said, "Ah, Warwick, why have you withdrawn yourself? Your bastard brother's blood — not the blood of the Marquess of Montague — the thirsty earth has drunk after the steely point of Clifford's lance pierced him like a wine cask. And in the very pangs of death he cried, like a dismal clangor heard from afar, 'Warwick, revenge! Brother, revenge my death!' So, underneath the belly of their steeds that stained their fetlocks in his steaming blood, the noble gentleman gave up the ghost."

Enraged, the Earl of Warwick cried, "Then let the earth become drunken with our blood! I'll kill my horse because I will not flee! Why do we stand here like soft-hearted women, bewailing our losses, while the foe rages? Why do we look upon these events as if the tragedy were played in jest by counterfeiting, feigning actors?"

He knelt and said, "Here on my knee I vow to God above, I'll never pause again, never stand still, until either death has closed these eyes of mine or Lady Fortune has given me my measure — my share — of revenge."

Duke Edward of York knelt and said, "Oh, Warwick, I bend my knee with yours, and in this vow I chain my soul to yours!

"And, before my knee rises from the earth's cold face, I throw my hands, my eyes, my heart to You, God, You setter up and plucker down of Kings. I beseech You that if with Your will it stands that this body must be prey to my foes, yet may your strong gates of Heaven open and give sweet passage inside to my sinful soul!

Daniel 2:21 states, "*And he changeth the times and seasons: he taketh away kings: he setteth up kings: he giveth wisdom unto the wise, and understanding to those that understand*" (1599 Geneva Bible).

Duke Edward of York continued, "Now, lords, let us take leave until we meet again, wherever it be, in Heaven or on Earth."

Richard said, "Brother, give me your hand, and gentle Warwick, let me embrace you in my weary arms. I, who never did weep, now melt with woe that winter should cut off our springtime so."

"Let's go! Let's go!" the Earl of Warwick said. "Once more, sweet lords, farewell."

George said, "Yet let us all together go to our troops and give permission to flee to those who will not stay. And let us call them pillars who will stand by and support us; we will promise them such rewards as victors wear at the Olympian games if we thrive. This may plant courage in their quailing breasts, for yet there is hope of life and victory. Delay no longer; let's go away from here at full speed."

In another part of the battlefield, Richard and Lord Clifford met.

Richard said, "Now, Clifford, I have singled you out of the herd so that you are alone and I can hunt you. Suppose this arm of mine is for the Duke of York, and this arm of mine is for Rutland. Both of my arms are under an obligation to get revenge even if you were surrounded by a strong bronze wall."

"Now, Richard, I am with you here alone," Lord Clifford replied. "This is the hand that stabbed your father York, and this is the hand that slew your brother Rutland, and here's the heart that triumphs and exults in their death and cheers these hands that slew your sire and brother to execute the same slaughter upon yourself. And so, let's fight!"

They fought, but the Earl of Warwick arrived. Unwilling to fight both Richard and the Earl of Warwick, one against two, Lord Clifford fled.

Richard said, "No, Warwick, single out some other game to hunt, for I myself will hunt this wolf to death."

Richard ran after Lord Clifford.

In another part of the battlefield, King Henry VI said to himself, "This battle fares like the morning's war, when dying clouds contend with growing light at that time the shepherd, blowing on his fingernails to warm his hands, can call it neither perfect day nor perfect night.

"Now sways the morning's war this way, like a mighty sea forced by the tide to combat with the wind. Now sways it that way, like the selfsame sea forced to retire by the fury of the wind. Sometimes the flood prevails, and then the wind prevails. Now one is the better, and then another is best. Both are tugging to be victors, breast to breast, yet neither is conqueror nor conquered, and so the morning's war is the equal of this deadly war.

"Here on this molehill I will sit down.

"To whom God will, there be the victory! My Queen Margaret and Clifford, too, have scolded me and shooed me away from the battle, both of them swearing that they prosper best of all when I am absent.

"I wish that I were dead — if God's good will would have it so — for what is in this world but grief and woe?

"Oh, God! I think it would be a happy life to be no better than a simple shepherd, to sit upon a hill, as I do now, to artfully carve out sundials in the turf of a hillside, point by point, thereby to see how the minutes run, how many minutes make the hour fully complete, how many hours bring about the day, how many days will finish up the year, and how many years a mortal man may live.

"When this is known, then to divide the times: So many hours must I tend my flock, so many hours must I take my rest, so many hours must I contemplate and pray, so many hours must I entertain myself, so many days my ewes have been with young, so many weeks before the poor fools will give birth, and so many years before I shall shear the fleece.

"In this way, minutes, hours, days, months, and years would pass over to the purpose for which they were created, and they would bring white hairs to a quiet grave.

"Ah, what a life would this be! How sweet! How lovely!

"Doesn't the hawthorn bush give a sweeter shade to shepherds looking on their defenseless sheep than a rich embroidered canopy does to Kings who fear their subjects' treachery? Oh, yes, it does — a thousand-fold it does.

"And to conclude, the shepherd's homely curds, his cold, thin drink out of his leather bottle, his usual sleep under a fresh tree's shade, all of which he enjoys securely and sweetly, is far beyond a Prince's delicacies, his food sparkling in a golden cup, his body couched in a finely wrought bed, when care, mistrust, and treason lie in wait for him."

A trumpet sounded a battle call.

Two soldiers arrived and fought. The younger soldier killed the older soldier.

The younger soldier said, "Ill blows the wind that profits nobody. This man, whom hand to hand I slew in fight, may be possessed with some store of coins, and I, who happen to take them from him now, may yet before night yield both my life and the coins to some other man, as this dead man does to me."

He took the older soldier's helmet off and said, "Who's this? Oh, God! It is the face of my father, whom in this conflict I have killed without knowing who he was.

"Oh, heavy, sorrowful times, begetting such events! From London I was impressed by the King into the King's army. My father, being the Earl of Warwick's man, came here to fight on the side of the Duke of York after being impressed by his master into the Duke's army.

"And I, who at my father's hands received my life, have by my hands bereaved him of life.

"Pardon me, God. I knew not what I did! And pardon me, father, for I did not know who you were!

"My tears shall wipe away these bloody marks on my father's face, and I will say no more words until my tears have flowed their fill."

King Henry VI said, "Oh, piteous spectacle! Oh, bloody times! While lions war and battle for their dens, poor harmless lambs endure their enmity.

"Weep, wretched man, I'll aid you tear for tear, and let our hearts and eyes, like civil war, be blind with tears, and break overburdened with grief."

Two more soldiers arrived and fought. The older soldier killed the younger soldier.

The older soldier said, "You who so bravely have resisted me, give me your gold, if you have any gold, for I have bought it with a hundred blows."

He took the younger soldier's helmet off and said, "But let me see. Is this our foeman's face? Ah, no, no, no, it is the face of my only son!

"Ah, boy, if any life is left in you, open your eyes! See, see what showers arise, blown with the windy tempest of my heart, upon your wounds that kill my eyes and heart!

"Oh, pity, God, this miserable age! What bloodthirsty deeds, how deadly, how butcherly, criminal, mutinous and unnatural and abnormal, this deadly quarrel daily begets!

"Oh, boy, your father gave you life too soon, and he has bereft you of your life too late!

"Oh, boy, your father gave you life too soon because you are old enough to be a soldier, and he has lived too long — because he lived long enough to just now bereft you of your life late in his own life!"

King Henry VI said, "Woe above woe! Grief more than common grief! I wish that my death would stop these piteous deeds! Oh, pity, pity, gentle Heaven, have pity!

"The red rose and the white rose are on his face, the fatal colors of our striving Houses. The one his red blood very well resembles; the other his pale cheeks, I think, present. May one rose wither and let the other rose flourish. If the red rose and the white rose fight, a thousand lives must wither."

The son who had killed his father said, "How my mother will be angry with me because of a father's death and never be happy again!"

The father who had killed his son said, "How my wife will shed seas of tears because of the slaughter of my son and never be happy again!"

King Henry VI said, "How the country because of these woeful occurrences will think ill of the King and not be happy!"

The son who had killed his father said, "Has a son ever so rued a father's death?"

The father who had killed his son said, "Has a father ever so mourned his son?"

King Henry VI said, "Has a King ever so grieved for subjects' woe? Much is your sorrow; mine is ten times as much."

The son who had killed his father said, "I'll carry you away to a place where I may weep my fill."

He exited, carrying his father's corpse.

The father who had killed his son said, "These arms of mine shall be your shroud. My heart, sweet boy, shall be your sepulcher, for from my heart your image shall never go. My sighing breast shall be your funeral bell, and so dutiful in performing your funeral rites will your father be, even for the loss of you, my only son, as Priam was for all his valiant sons."

Priam, King of Troy, lost many of his fifty sons during the Trojan War.

The father who had killed his son continued, "I'll carry you away from here, and let them fight who will, for I have murdered where I should not kill."

He exited, carrying his son's corpse.

King Henry VI said, "Sad-hearted men, much overcome with cares and concerns, here sits a King more woeful than you are."

Queen Margaret, Prince Edward, and the Duke of Exeter arrived.

Prince Edward said to King Henry VI, "Flee, father, flee! For all your friends have fled, and Warwick rages like an angry bull! Run away! Death pursues us!"

"Mount on horseback, my lord," Queen Margaret said. "Ride towards Berwick-on-Tweed in Northumberland as quickly as you can. Edward and Richard, like a pair of greyhounds that have the fearful, fleeing hare in sight, with their fiery eyes sparkling with thorough-going wrath, and bloody steel swords grasped in their angry hands, are at our backs, and therefore you need to go away from here as quickly as possible."

The Duke of Exeter said, "Run away! For vengeance comes along with them. No, don't cause delay by speaking; make a speedy exit now, or else follow me later. I'm going now."

"No, take me with you, good sweet Exeter," King Henry VI said. "Not that I fear to stay, but that I love to go wherever the Queen journeys. Forward; let's go!"

In another part of the battlefield, an injured Lord Clifford knew he was dying.

Alone, he said, "Here burns my candle out; yes, here it dies. My candle, while it lasted, gave the Lancastrian King Henry VI light.

"Oh, House of Lancaster, I fear your overthrow more than my body's parting with my soul! Love and fear of me glued many friends to you, and now that I am falling, your tough commixture melts — your strong alliances dissolve.

"Impairing Henry and strengthening wickedly proud York, the common people swarm like summer flies; and where do gnats fly but to the Sun? And who shines now but Henry's enemies?

"Oh, Phoebus Apollo — Henry — if you had never given consent that Phaëthon — the Duke of York — should control your fiery steeds, your burning Sun-chariot would never have scorched the Earth!

"And, Henry, had you ruled as Kings should do, or as your father and his father did, giving no ground to the House of York, they never then had sprung up like summer flies. I and ten thousand other men in this luckless realm would not have left any widows mourning for our death, and you this day would have kept your throne in peace.

"For what nourishes weeds but gentle air? And what makes robbers bold but too much lenity?

"But useless are my complaints, and incurable are my wounds. I have no way to flee, nor do I have the strength to sustain flight.

"The foe is merciless, and will not pity me, for at their hands I have deserved no pity. The air has gotten into my fatal wounds, and much shedding of blood makes me faint.

"Come, York and Richard, Warwick and the rest. I stabbed your fathers' bosoms; now split my breast."

He fainted.

A trumpet called the Lancastrian army to retreat, leaving the Yorkist army triumphant.

The Yorkists Edward, George, Richard, the Marquess of Montague, and the Earl of Warwick arrived. Some Yorkist soldiers were with them.

Edward said, "Now we rest, lords. Good fortune bids us pause and smooth the frowns of war with peaceful looks.

"Some troops pursue the bloodthirsty-minded Queen, who led calm Henry, although he were a King, as a sail, filled with a fretting gust, commands and forces an argosy — a large merchant ship — to make headway against the waves.

"But, lords, do you think that Lord Clifford fled with them?"

"No, it is impossible that he should escape," the Earl of Warwick said, "for although before your brother Richard's face I speak the words, Richard marked him for the grave, and wherever Lord Clifford is, he's surely dead."

Lord Clifford groaned and died.

Edward said, "Whose soul is that which takes its sorrowful departure?"

Richard said, "A deadly groan, like life departing and leaving death."

"See who it is," Edward said, "and now the battle's ended, whether he is friend or foe, let him be gently treated."

Richard looked at the corpse and said, "Revoke that sentence of mercy, for it is Clifford, who not contented that he lopped the branch in hewing Rutland when his leaves put forth, set his murdering knife to the root from whence that tender spray did sweetly spring. I mean that Lord Clifford murdered our Princely father, the Duke of York."

The Earl of Warwick said, "From off the gates of York fetch down your father's head, which Clifford placed there. Instead, let this head take its place. Measure must be repaid with measure. An eye for an eye; a tooth for a tooth."

Edward said about Lord Clifford's body, "Bring forth that fatal screech owl to our house, that owl that sang nothing but death to us and ours. Now death shall stop his dismal threatening sound, and his ill-boding tongue no more shall speak."

The Earl of Warwick looked at Lord Clifford's body and said, "I think his understanding has left him.

"Speak, Clifford, do you know who is speaking to you?

"Dark, cloudy death casts a gloom over his beams of life, and he neither sees us nor hears what we say."

"Oh, I wish he did!" Richard said. "And so perhaps he does. Perhaps it is just his trick and he is pretending to be dead because he wants to avoid such bitter taunts as those that he gave our father in his time of death."

George said, "If you think so, then vex him with sharp, cutting words."

"Clifford, ask for mercy and obtain no grace," Richard said.

"Clifford, repent in unavailing penitence," Edward said.

The Earl of Warwick said, "Clifford, make excuses for your crimes and sins —"

"— while we devise cruel tortures for your crimes and sins," George said.

"You 'loved' York," Richard said, "and I am a son of the old Duke of York."

"You 'pitied' Rutland," Edward said. "I will 'pity' you."

"Where's Captain Margaret, to protect you now?" George asked.

"They mock you, Clifford," the Earl of Warwick said. "Swear as you were accustomed to swear."

"What, no oath!" Richard said. "The world goes hard when Clifford cannot spare his 'friends' an oath. I know by that he's dead, and by my soul, if this right hand could buy two hours of life for him, so that I in all contempt might rail at him, this hand would chop off my other hand, and with the blood that spurts out I would choke and strangle and drown this villain whose unquenchable thirst for blood the deaths of the old Duke of York and young Rutland could not satisfy."

"Yes, he's dead," the Earl of Warwick said. "Off with the traitor's head, and put it in the place where your father's head now stands. And now triumphantly march to London, where you will be crowned England's royal King: Edward IV. From London I, Warwick, will cut the sea to France, and ask for the Lady Bona, sister-in-law of the King of France to be your Queen. With that marriage, you shall strongly join, as with a sinew, both these lands — England and France — together. And, having the King of France as your friend, you shall not dread the scattered foes — the Lancastrians — who hope to rise again. For although they cannot greatly sting to hurt, yet look to have them buzz to offend your ears. They will circulate rumors about you.

"First I will see the coronation, and then I'll cross the sea to Brittany to bring about this marriage, if it pleases my lord."

"Do as you will, sweet Warwick," Edward said. "Let it be done, for with your strong shoulder as my support I build my throne, and I will never undertake the thing for which your counsel and consent are lacking.

"Richard, I will make you Duke of Gloucester, and George, I will make you Duke of Clarence."

Using the royal plural, he said, "Warwick, with the consent of and acting as ourself, shall do and undo as pleases him best."

Richard joked, "Let me be the Duke of Clarence, and let George be the Duke of Gloucester because Gloucester's Dukedom is too ominous. The previous three Dukes of Gloucester have died violent deaths."

The Earl of Warwick said, "Tut, that's a foolish observation. Richard, you will be the Duke of Gloucester. Now let's go to London to see to the rituals that will give all of you possession of these honors."

CHAPTER 3

— 3.1 —

In a rural area in the north of England, two gamekeepers carrying crossbows were talking.

The first gamekeeper said, "Under this thickly grown thicket, we'll shroud and hide ourselves, for through this glade the deer will soon come, and in this covert we will make our hiding place and choose the best of all the deer."

"I'll stay higher up the hill, so both of us may shoot," the second gamekeeper said.

"That cannot be," the first gamekeeper said. "The noise of your crossbow will scare the herd of deer, and so my shot will be lost. Here we both will stand, and we will aim at the best deer. So that the time shall not seem tedious, I'll tell you what befell me on a day in this same place where now we intend to stand."

The second gamekeeper looked up and said, "Here comes a man; let's wait until he has passed by."

King Henry VI, disguised and carrying a prayer book, was the man the second gamekeeper had seen.

King Henry VI said, "From Scotland I have stolen, purely out of love, to greet my own land with my wistful sight. No, Harry, Harry, it is no land of yours. Your place is filled, your scepter has been wrung from you, and the balm with which you were anointed has been washed off. No bending knee will call you Caesar now, no humble petitioners will press forward to speak to you and ask you for justice. No, not a man comes to you for redress of wrongs, for how can I help them, when I cannot help myself?"

The first gamekeeper said, "Aye, here's a deer whose skin's a gamekeeper's fee. This is the former King; let's seize him."

Gamekeepers received the skin and head of a deer in payment for their services.

"Let me embrace you, sour adversity," King Henry VI said, "for wise men say it is the wisest course."

"Why do we linger?" the second gamekeeper said. "Let us lay hands on him."

"Wait awhile," the first gamekeeper said. "We'll listen a little longer."

King Henry VI said, "My Queen and son have gone to the King of France to seek aid, and I hear that the great commanding Earl of Warwick has also gone thither to request the French King's sister-in-law as a wife for Edward, son of the late Duke of York. If this news is true, then, the labor of my poor Queen and son is only lost, for Warwick is a subtle orator and King Louis XI is a Prince soon won with moving words.

"However, by this second point — King Louis XI is a Prince soon won with moving words — Margaret may win him, for she's a woman to be much pitied. Her sighs will make an assault on his breast. Her tears will pierce into a marble heart. The tiger will be mild while she mourns, and even a cruel tyrant such as the Roman emperor Nero will be affected by remorse when he hears her complaints and sees her brinish tears.

"Yes, but she's come to beg, while Warwick has come to give. Margaret, on the French King's left side, will beg for aid for me, Henry. Warwick, on his right side, will ask for a wife for Edward — a good marriage for the French King's sister-in-law. "

King Henry VI continued to speak, mentioning the Edward who was a member of the York family. He did not mention Edward, his own son who was the Prince of Wales:

"Margaret will weep and say that her Henry has been deposed. Warwick will smile and say that his Edward has been formally installed as King of England.

"She, poor wretch, will be able to speak no more because of grief, while Warwick will tell the French King about Edward's claim to be King of England. Warwick will smoothly pass over the wrong that Edward has done in claiming the crown and he will put forth arguments of mighty strength, and in conclusion he will win the King of France away from Margaret with the promise of a good marriage for his sister-in-law, and who knows what else he will say to strengthen and support King Edward IV's place on the throne.

"Oh, Margaret, thus it will be, and you, poor soul, will then be forsaken because you went forlorn to the King of France!"

The gamekeepers came out of hiding.

The second gamekeeper said, "Tell us who you are who talks of Kings and Queens."

King Henry VI said, "I am more than I seem, and less than I was born to. I am a man at least, for less I should not be. Men may talk of Kings, and so why not I?"

The second gamekeeper said, "Yes, but you talk as if you were a King."

"Why, so I am, in my mind, and that's enough," King Henry VI said.

"But, if you are a King, then where is your crown?" the second gamekeeper asked.

"My crown is in my heart, not on my head," King Henry VI said. "My crown is not decorated with diamonds and jewels from India, nor is it to be seen. My crown is called contentment: It is a crown that Kings seldom enjoy."

The second gamekeeper said, "Well, if you are a King crowned with contentment, your crown of contentment and you must be contented to go along with us, for we think that you are the King whom King Edward IV has deposed, and we his subjects sworn in all allegiance will apprehend you as his enemy."

"Haven't you ever sworn and broken an oath?" King Henry VI asked.

"No, I never have, and I will not now," the second gamekeeper said.

"Where did you dwell when I was King of England?"

"Here in this country, where we now remain," the second gamekeeper replied.

"I was anointed King at nine months old," King Henry VI said. "My father and my grandfather were Kings, and you were sworn true subjects to me. Tell me, then, haven't you broken your oaths?"

"No, for we were your subjects only while you were King," the first gamekeeper said.

"Am I dead?" King Henry VI said. "Don't I breathe as a living man? Ah, simple men, you know not what you swear!"

He picked up a feather from the ground and said, "Look as I blow this feather from my face, and look as the air blows it to me again; the feather obeys my wind when I blow, and yields to another wind when it blows, commanded always by the greater gust. Such is the lightness and fickleness of you common men.

"But do not break your oaths, for of that sin my mild entreaty shall not make you guilty. Go where you will; the King shall be commanded. You two be the Kings: Command, and I'll obey."

The first gamekeeper said, "We are true and loyal subjects to the King of England: King Edward IV."

"So would you be again to Henry VI, if he were seated on the throne as King Edward IV is," King Henry VI said.

"We order you, in God's name, and the King's, to go with us to the officers of the peace," the first gamekeeper said.

"In God's name, lead," King Henry VI said. "May your King's name be obeyed, and whatever God wills, let your King perform, and whatever he wills, I humbly yield to."

King Edward IV, Duke Richard of Gloucester, Duke George of Clarence, and Lady Elizabeth Grey were together in a room in the palace at London. Richard and George had recently become Dukes.

King Edward IV said, "Brother Richard of Gloucester, at Saint Albans' battlefield this lady's husband, Sir Richard Grey, was slain. His lands were then seized by the conqueror. Her petition to me is now to allow her to repossess those lands, which we in justice cannot well deny because the worthy gentleman lost his life on the side of the House of York."

Duke Richard of Gloucester said, "Your highness shall do well to grant her petition. It would be dishonorable to deny it."

"It would be no less than dishonorable, but yet I'll pause before I make a decision," King Edward IV said.

Both Duke Richard of Gloucester and Duke George of Clarence knew that King Edward IV was sexually attracted to Lady Elizabeth Grey.

Duke Richard of Gloucester whispered to Duke George of Clarence, "Is that so? I see the lady has a thing to grant, before the King will grant her humble petition."

In this culture, the word "thing" also meant genitals. Richard meant that before King Edward IV would grant Lady Elizabeth Grey her lands, she would have to grant him access to her vagina.

Duke George of Clarence whispered to Richard, "He knows the game. How well he keeps downwind so she doesn't immediately smell what he wants!"

"Silence!" Richard whispered to Duke George of Clarence.

King Edward IV said, "Widow, we will consider your petition; come back some other time to know what we have decided."

"Right gracious lord, I cannot endure delay," Lady Elizabeth Grey replied. "May it please your highness to tell me what your decision is now? Whatever your pleasure is, it shall satisfy me."

Her words had a sexual meaning of which she was unaware. She was unknowingly saying that the King's sexual pleasure would satisfy her — by having sex with King Edward IV, she would receive the satisfaction of getting her late husband's lands back.

Duke Richard of Gloucester whispered to Duke George of Clarence, "Is that so, widow? Then I'll warrant that you will get all your lands, if what pleases him shall pleasure you. Fight closer, or, in good faith, you'll catch a blow. Fight more closely if you want to avoid his thrusts."

The blows — thrusts — could be made in fencing, or in bed.

Lady Elizabeth Grey had the chance to "fight" closer to King Edward IV in bed so that she could avoid the blow of not receiving her husband's lands.

Duke George of Clarence whispered to Richard, "I am not afraid for her, unless she should happen to fall."

One kind of fall would be into bed.

Duke Richard of Gloucester whispered to Duke George of Clarence, "May God forbid that! For the King will take advantage."

King Edward IV asked Lady Elizabeth Grey, "How many children do you have, widow? Tell me."

Duke George of Clarence whispered to Richard, "I think he means to beg a child of her."

"To beg a child of her" could mean 1) "to beg that he be allowed to make one of her children his ward," or 2) "to beg that she give birth to one of his future biological children."

Duke Richard of Gloucester whispered to Duke George of Clarence, "No, if that happens, whip me. He'd rather make her pregnant twice and give her two children."

Lady Elizabeth Grey said to King Edward IV, "I have three children, my most gracious lord."

Duke Richard of Gloucester whispered to Duke George of Clarence, "She shall have four, if she'll be ruled by the King."

King Edward IV said, "It would be a pity if they would lose their father's lands."

"Be full of pity, revered lord, and grant my petition then," Lady Elizabeth Grey said.

King Edward IV asked his two brothers, Richard and Duke George of Clarence, "Lords, give us good leave — let the widow and I speak together privately. I'll test this widow's moral and mental sharpness."

As they walked a short distance away, Richard said to Duke George of Clarence about Edward, "Aye, good leave have you, for you will have leave until your youth takes leave and leaves you to the crutch — and crotch — of old age."

"Good leave" is "good permission." Richard was saying that King Edward IV would use his position of power to get much permission from women to have sex with them until he got too old to have sex.

King Edward IV said, "Now tell me, madam, do you love your children?"

"Yes," Lady Elizabeth Grey replied. "I love them fully as dearly as I love myself."

"And would you not do much to do them good?" King Edward IV asked.

One meaning of the word "do" is "f**k."

"To do them good, I would sustain some harm," Lady Elizabeth Grey replied.

"Then get your husband's lands, to do them good," King Edward IV said.

"That's why I have come to your majesty," Lady Elizabeth Grey said.

"I'll tell you how these lands are to be gotten," King Edward IV said.

"If you do, you shall bind me to your highness' service," Lady Elizabeth Grey replied.

"What service will you do me, if I give you the lands?" King Edward IV asked.

He meant sexual service.

"Whatever you command that rests in me to do," Lady Elizabeth Grey replied.

"But you will take exception to my request," King Edward IV said.

"No, gracious lord, with the exception that I cannot do your request," Lady Elizabeth Grey replied.

"Aye, but you can do what I mean to ask," King Edward IV said.

"Why, then I will do what your grace commands," Lady Elizabeth Grey said.

Duke Richard of Gloucester and Duke George of Clarence were watching, but they could not hear.

Richard whispered to Duke George of Clarence, "He plies her hard, and much rain wears the marble."

Duke George of Clarence said to Richard, "The King is horny! His sexual excitement makes him as red as fire! Her wax must melt in the presence of his fire. She will grow wet."

Lady Elizabeth Grey said, "Why did my lord stop speaking? Shall I not hear the task you want me to do?"

"It is an easy task," King Edward IV said. "It is only to love a King."

"That's soon performed, because I am a subject, and subjects love their King," Lady Elizabeth Grey said.

"Why, then, your husband's lands I freely give you," King Edward IV said.

"I take my leave with many thousand thanks," Lady Elizabeth Gray said.

Richard believed that Lady Elizabeth Grey had agreed to sleep with the King.

Richard whispered to Duke George of Clarence, "The match is made; she seals it with a curtsy."

"Wait," King Edward IV said, "it is the fruits of love I mean."

He meant sex, which sometimes results in the fruit of the womb.

"I also mean the fruits of love, my loving liege," Lady Elizabeth Grey said.

She meant the love and respect that a loyal subject had for his or her King.

King Edward IV said, "Yes, but I am afraid that you are using the words in another sense than I am. What love do you think I am pursuing so much?"

"My love until I die, my humble thanks, my prayers," Lady Elizabeth Grey replied. "That love which virtue begs and virtue grants."

"No, by my truth, I did not mean such love," King Edward IV said.

"Why, then you did not mean what I thought you did," Lady Elizabeth Grey said, realizing what he wanted.

"But now you may partly perceive my mind," King Edward IV said.

"My mind will never grant what I perceive your highness aims at, if I aim — guess — rightly," Lady Elizabeth Grey said.

"To tell you plainly, I aim to lie with you in bed," King Edward IV said.

"To tell you plainly, I had rather lie in prison," Lady Elizabeth Grey said.

"Why, then you shall not have your late husband's lands," King Edward IV said.

"Why, then my chastity shall be my dower," Lady Elizabeth Grey said, "for I will not purchase my late husband's lands with the loss of my chastity."

A dower is a widow's share of her late husband's estate.

"Therein you wrong your children mightily," King Edward IV said.

"Herein your highness wrongs both them and me," Lady Elizabeth Grey said. "But, mighty lord, this merry inclination of yours is not in accord with the seriousness of my petition to you. Please dismiss me with either 'yes' or 'no.'"

"Yes, if you will say 'yes' to my request," King Edward IV replied. "No if you say 'no' to my demand."

"Then, no, my lord," Lady Elizabeth Grey said. "My petition to you is at an end."

Duke Richard of Gloucester whispered to Duke George of Clarence, "The widow does not like him; she knits her eyebrows and frowns."

George whispered to Richard, "The King is the bluntest and most unceremonious wooer in all Christendom."

King Edward IV thought, *Her angry looks in response to my proposition show that she is replete with modesty. Her words show that her intelligence is incomparable. All her perfections have a natural claim on sovereignty. One way or other, she is for a King, and she shall be my lover, or else my Queen.*

He said out loud, "Suppose that King Edward IV takes you for his Queen?"

"It is better said than done, my gracious lord," Lady Elizabeth Grey replied. "I am a subject fit to jest with, but I am very unfit to be a sovereign."

"Sweet widow, by my sovereignty I swear to you that I say no more than what my soul intends," King Edward IV replied, "and that is, to enjoy you for my love."

"And that is more than I will yield to," Lady Elizabeth Grey said. "I know I am too mean — too low in social status — to be your Queen, and yet I am too good to be your concubine."

"You cavil, widow," King Edward IV said. "I did mean that I want you to be my Queen."

"It will grieve your grace that my sons would call you father," Lady Elizabeth Grey said.

"No more than when my daughters call you mother," King Edward IV replied. "You are a widow, and you have some children. And, by God's mother, I, who am only a bachelor, have some other children. Both of us are fertile. Why, it is a happy thing to be the father to many sons.

"Say no more and make no more objections, for you shall be my Queen."

Richard whispered to Duke George of Clarence, "The ghostly father now has done his shrift. The priest has imposed his penance and performed his absolution."

Duke George of Clarence whispered to Richard, "When he was made a shriver, it was for shift."

"Ghostly" meant "spiritual." A shriver is a father confessor. A shift is a woman's undergarment. A joke of the time was to say that a woman had been "shriven to her shift" — that is, seduced.

King Edward IV walked over to his two brothers and said, "Brothers, you must wonder what Lady Elizabeth Grey and I have been talking about."

Duke Richard of Gloucester said, "The widow did not like it, for she looks very serious."

"You'll think it strange if I would marry her," King Edward IV said.

"Marry her to whom, my lord?" Duke George of Clarence asked. Kings often had the right to marry nobles to each other.

"Why, Clarence, to myself," King Edward IV said.

"That would be ten days' wonder at the least," Duke Richard of Gloucester said.

"That's a day longer than a wonder lasts," Duke George of Clarence said.

A cliché of the time was "nine days' wonder."

"By so much is this an extreme wonder," Richard said.

"Well, jest on, brothers," King Edward IV said. "I can tell you both that I have granted her suit to gain possession of her late husband's lands."

A nobleman entered the room and said, "My gracious lord, your foe Henry VI has been captured. He has been brought as your prisoner to your palace gate."

"See that he is conveyed to the Tower of London," King Edward IV said, "and let's go, brothers, to the man who captured him to question him about how he captured Henry.

"Widow, come along with us.

"Lords, treat her honorably."

Everyone left except Duke Richard of Gloucester, who said to himself, "Yes, Edward will use women honorably. He will use a woman and be on-her-ably. I wish that he were wasted, marrow, bones, and all, with venereal disease so that from his loins no hopeful branch may spring and be born to cross and thwart me from accomplishing the golden time of wearing a golden crown I look for!

"And yet, between my soul's desire and me — once the lustful Edward's title of being King of England is dead and buried — is my older brother Duke George of Clarence, Henry VI, and Henry VI's son, who is young Edward, as well as all the unwelcome children they will sire. These will all have precedence before I can be King. This is a cold forecast for accomplishing my goal!

"Why, then, I only dream about sovereignty and being King. I am like a person who stands upon a promontory and spies a far-off shore where he wants to tread. He wishes that his feet could travel there as quickly as his eye, and so he curses the sea that separates him from where he wants to be, saying that he'll ladle it dry to make his passage.

"Just like that, I wish I had the crown, which is so far off, and so I curse the obstacles that keep me from it, and so I say that I'll remove the obstacles by cutting their lives short, thereby flattering myself with impossibilities.

"My eye is too quick and my heart presumes too much, unless my hand and strength could equal them.

"Well, let's say there is no Kingdom then for Richard. What other pleasure can the world afford? I'll make my Heaven in a lady's vagina, and deck my body in gay ornamental clothing, and bewitch sweet ladies with my words and looks.

"Oh, miserable thought! To do that is more unlikely than to accomplish the acquisition of twenty golden crowns!

"Why, the goddess Love forswore me when I was in my mother's womb, and in order that I should not deal in her soft laws of love, she corrupted frail nature with some bribe to shrink my arm up like a withered shrub, to make out of spite a mountain on my back — where sits deformity to mock my body — to make my legs of an unequal size, and to make me disproportionate in every part, as if I were a chaos, or an unlicked bear-whelp that has no resemblance to its dam."

In this culture, people believed that when bear cubs were born they were unshaped masses and their mother bear licked them into the proper shape.

Richard continued, "And am I then a man to be beloved? Oh, monstrous fault, to harbor such a thought!

"Then, since this earth affords no joy to me, except to command, to restrain and rebuke, to overrule and overcome such as are of better physical appearance than myself, I'll make my Heaven to dream upon the crown, and while I live, I will consider this world only a Hell, until my misshapen trunk that bears this head be surrounded with a glorious crown.

"And yet I don't know how to get the crown because many lives stand between me and my goal. And I — like one lost in a thorny wood, one who rends the thorns and is rent by the thorns, seeking a way and straying from the way; not knowing how to find the open air, but toiling desperately to find it — torment myself to catch the English crown.

"And from that torment I will free myself, or hew my way out with a bloody axe.

"Why, I can smile, and murder while I smile. And I can cry 'I am content' to that which grieves my heart, and wet my cheeks with artificial tears, and frame my face to all occasions.

"I'll drown more sailors than the mermaids known as the Sirens shall."

The Sirens used their beautiful singing voices to entice sailors to come too close to shore and wreck their ships.

Richard continued, "I'll slay more gazers than the basilisk."

The basilisk is a mythological serpent that can kill with its look.

Richard continued, "I'll play the orator as well as Nestor, deceive more slyly than Ulysses could, and like a Sinon, conquer another Troy."

Nestor was the wise old advisor to Agamemnon, leader of the Greek army against Troy. Ulysses' Greek name was Odysseus. He was the trickiest of all the Greeks and is the hero of Homer's *Odyssey*. Ulysses came up with the idea of the Trojan Horse, which Sinon convinced the Trojans to take into the city. London was considered a new Troy because people believed that a grandson of the Trojan hero Aeneas had founded it.

Richard continued, "I can add colors to the chameleon, change shapes with Proteus for advantages, and set the murderous Machiavelli to school."

The chameleon can change colors so that it remains unseen. Proteus was a shape-shifter. Machiavelli was an Italian political theorist who was widely regarded as completely lacking morality.

Richard continued, "Can I do this, and cannot get a crown? Tut, even if it were farther off, I'll pluck it down."

A number of people were meeting in a room of King Louis XI's palace in Paris: King Louis XI of France, his sister-in-law Lady Bona, the French Admiral Bourbon, Prince Edward of England, Queen Margaret, and the Earl of Oxford, one of King Henry VI's supporters.

King Louis XI said, "Fair Queen of England, worthy Margaret, sit down with us. It ill befits your royal position and lineage that you should stand while I, Louis, sit."

"No, mighty King of France," Queen Margaret replied. "Now Margaret must strike her sail and learn for a while to serve where Kings command."

A lowlier vessel would strike — lower — its sail in deference to a mightier ship. Striking the sail was also used as a sign that the ship was surrendering.

Queen Margaret continued, "I was, I must confess, great Albion's Queen in former golden days."

"Albion" is an ancient name for Britain.

She continued, "But now misfortune has trodden my title of Queen down, and with dishonor laid me on the ground, where I must take a low seat that is like my low fortune, and I must bring myself into conformity with my humble seat."

"Tell me, fair Queen, from what springs this deep despair?" King Louis XI asked.

"From such a cause as fills my eyes with tears and stops my tongue, while my heart is drowned in cares," Queen Margaret said.

"Whatever that cause is, always be royalty like yourself, and sit yourself by our side," he said, using the royal plural.

They sat down, and the King of France added, "Don't allow your neck to yield to the yoke of fortune, but instead let your dauntless mind always ride in triumph over all misfortune.

"Be plainspoken, Queen Margaret, and tell me about your grief. It shall be eased, if the King of France can yield relief."

Queen Margaret replied, "Those gracious words revive my drooping thoughts and give my tongue-tied sorrows permission and the ability to speak. Now, therefore, be it known to noble Louis, that Henry VI, sole possessor of my love, from being a King has become a banished man, and he is forced to live in Scotland as a forlorn man, while proud, ambitious Edward, Duke of York, usurps the regal title and the seat of England's truly anointed and lawful King.

"This is the reason that I, poor Margaret, with this my son, Prince Edward, King Henry VI's heir, have come to request your just and lawful aid, and if you fail us, all our hope is over.

"Scotland wants to help, but cannot help. Our common people and our noble peers are both misled, our treasury has been seized, our soldiers put to flight, and as you see, we ourselves are in a heavy plight."

"Renowned Queen, use patience to calm the storm of your emotions, while we think about a means to bring the storm to an end," King Louis XI said.

"The more we delay, the stronger grows our foe," Queen Margaret said.

"The more I delay, the more I'll help you," King Louis XI said.

"Oh, but impatience waits on and serves true sorrow," Queen Margaret said.

The Earl of Warwick entered the room.

Queen Margaret said, "And see where comes the breeder — the cause — of my sorrow!"

"What is the rank of that man who boldly approaches our presence?" King Louis XI said.

Queen Margaret replied, "He is England's Earl of Warwick, Edward IV's greatest friend."

"Welcome, brave Warwick! What brings you to France?" King Louis XI said.

Both King Louis XI and Queen Margaret stood up, but only King Louis XI stepped down from the dias to greet the Earl of Warwick.

Queen Margaret thought, *Yes, now a second storm begins to rise, for this is the man who moves both wind and tide.*

The Earl of Warwick said to King Louis XI, "From worthy Edward IV, King of Albion, who is my lord and sovereign and your vowed friend, I come in kindness and unfeigned love, first to greet your royal person and then to ask for a league of friendship, and lastly to confirm that friendship with a nuptial knot, if you will grant that the virtuous Lady Bona, your fair sister-in-law, be given to England's King Edward IV in lawful marriage."

Queen Margaret thought, *If that happens, Henry VI's hope of regaining his crown is finished.*

The Earl of Warwick said to Lady Bona, "And, gracious madam, in our English King's behalf, I am commanded, with your permission and favor, humbly to kiss your hand, and with my tongue to tell you about the passion of my sovereign's heart, where reports about you, recently entering at his heedful ears, has placed your beauty's image and your virtue."

Queen Margaret said, "King Louis XI and Lady Bona, hear me speak before you give your answer to Warwick. His request does not spring from Edward IV's supposed well-meant honest love, but instead from deceit bred by necessity, for how can tyrants safely govern at home, unless they acquire great alliances abroad? To prove that Edward IV is a usurper, this may suffice: Henry VI is still alive, but even if he were dead, yet here Prince Edward, King Henry's son, stands.

"Be careful, therefore, Louis XI, that by this league and marriage you do not bring on yourself danger and dishonor, for although usurpers may rule for a while, yet the Heavens are just, and time suppresses wrongs."

"Insulting, slandering Margaret!" the Earl of Warwick said.

"And why do you not call her Queen?" Prince Edward asked.

The Earl of Warwick replied, "Because thy father, Henry VI, usurped the crown, and thou are Prince no more than she is Queen."

He deliberately used the — in this context — insulting "thy" and "thou" rather than the respectful "your" and "you."

The Earl of Oxford said, "Then Warwick makes null and nothing great John of Gaunt, who subdued the greatest part of Spain, and after John of Gaunt, King Henry IV, whose wisdom was a model of excellence to the wisest, and after wise King Henry IV, King Henry V, who by his prowess conquered all France. From these our King Henry VI lineally descends."

In his anger, the Earl of Oxford had brought up King Henry V's French conquests, something that King Louis XI did not want to hear about.

The Earl of Warwick replied, "Oxford, how does it happen that in this smooth discourse of yours, you did not mention that Henry VI has lost all that which Henry V had gotten? I think these peers of France should smile at that.

"But as for the rest, you tell a pedigree of threescore and two years."

Henry IV became King in 1399; Edward IV became King in 1461.

The Earl of Warwick continued, "That is a short time to make prescription for a Kingdom's worth."

The word "prescription" was used in a legal sense to mean "claim founded on long and uninterrupted use or possession."

The Earl of Oxford said, "Why, Warwick, can you speak against your liege, whom you obeyed for thirty-six years, and not reveal your treason with a blush?"

"Can Oxford, who always protected the right, now shield and protect falsehood with a pedigree? For shame! Leave Henry VI, and call Edward IV King."

The Earl of Oxford replied, "Call him my King by whose unjust and harmful order my elder brother, the Lord Aubrey Vere, was executed? And worse than that, he had my father killed — my father who was then in his old age and whom Nature had brought to the door of death?"

King Edward IV had executed them on a charge of treason.

The Earl of Oxford continued, "No, Warwick, no; while life upholds this arm, this arm upholds the House of Lancaster."

"And I uphold the House of York," the Earl of Warwick said.

King Louis XI said, "Queen Margaret, Prince Edward, and Oxford, please, at our request, stand aside while I have further conversation with Warwick."

Queen Margaret, Prince Edward, and the Earl of Oxford moved away far enough that they could not hear the French King's and Warwick's conversation.

Queen Margaret said to Prince Edward and the Earl of Oxford, "May the Heavens grant that Warwick's words do not bewitch King Louis XI!"

King Louis XI said, "Now Warwick, tell me, on your conscience, is Edward IV your true King? For I am loath to link myself with a King who was not lawfully chosen."

"On my reputation and my honor, I say that Edward IV is my true and lawfully chosen King," the Earl of Warwick replied.

"But is he popular and esteemed in the people's eye?" King Louis XI asked.

"The more that Henry VI is unfortunate, the more that Edward IV is esteemed."

"Tell me further — with all possible dissembling set aside — tell me truthfully the measure of Edward IV's love for our sister-in-law Lady Bona," King Louis XI said, using the royal plural.

"It is such as may befit a monarch like himself," the Earl of Warwick replied. "I myself have often heard him say and swear that this his love is an eternal plant, whereof the root is fixed in virtue's ground, the leaves and fruit maintained with beauty's Sun. His love will not feel the effects of malice because Lady Bona has no malice, but his love will feel the effects of disdain and rejection unless the Lady Bona removes his pain by returning his love."

King Louis XI said to Lady Bona, "Now, sister-in-law, let us hear your clear decision regarding marriage to the English King Edward IV."

"Your decision is my decision," Lady Bona replied. "Your agreement to, or your denial of, the marriage proposal will also be mine."

She then said to the Earl of Warwick, "Yet I confess that often before this day, when I have heard about your King Edward IV's merits, my ear has tempted my judgment to desire him."

King Louis XI, picking up on the implicit statement that she was willing to marry King Edward IV, said, "So then, Warwick, this is my decision: Our sister-in-law shall be Edward's wife, and now without delay the articles of the agreement shall be drawn up concerning the marriage settlement that your King must make. Her dower — what she will get if your King dies before she does — shall be matched by her dowry — what she brings to your King by marrying him."

He then said, "Draw near us, Queen Margaret, and be a witness that Lady Bona shall be the wife of the English King."

Prince Edward said, "She shall be married to Edward, who is called Edward IV, but not to the English King, who is my father."

"Deceitful Warwick!" Queen Margaret said. "It was your plot to make void my petition to Louis XI by making this alliance with him. Before you came here, Louis XI was Henry VI's friend."

King Louis XI said, "And he still is friends to Henry VI and Margaret, but if your claim to the crown is weak, as may appear by Edward IV's good success in obtaining the crown, then it is only reasonable that I be released from giving you the aid that just now I promised. Yet you shall have all kindness at my hand that your high rank requires and my estate can yield."

The Earl of Warwick said, "Henry VI now lives in Scotland at his ease, where since he has nothing, he can lose nothing. And as for you yourself, our former Queen, you have a father who is able to maintain you, and it would be better if you troubled him rather than the King of France."

"Be quiet, impudent and shameless Warwick, be quiet," Queen Margaret said. "Proud setter up and puller down of Kings! I will not leave from here until, with my talk and tears, both full of truth, I make King Louis XI see your sly trickery and your lord's false love, for both of you are birds of the same feather."

A horn sounded to announce the arrival of an express messenger.

King Louis XI said, "Warwick, this is some messenger to us or to you."

The messenger entered the room and gave a letter to the Earl of Warwick, saying, "My lord ambassador, this letter is for you, sent from your brother, the Marquess of Montague."

He gave King Louis XI a letter and said, "This letter is from our English King Edward IV to your majesty.

He gave Queen Margaret a letter and said, "This letter is for you; from whom it comes I don't know."

They all read their letters.

The Earl of Oxford said to Prince Edward, "I like it well that our fair Queen and leader smiles at her news, while the Earl of Warwick frowns at his."

Prince Edward replied, "Look at how King Louis XI stamps his foot as he were angry. I hope all's for the best."

King Louis XI asked, "Warwick, what is your news? And yours, fair Queen?"

Queen Margaret said, "My news is such as fills my heart with unhoped-for and unanticipated joys."

The Earl of Warwick said, "My news is full of sorrow and heart's discontent."

King Louis XI said, "Your King Edward IV has married the Lady Elizabeth Grey! And now, to smooth over your deceit and his, he has sent me a letter to persuade me to be calm and patient! Is this the alliance that he seeks with the King of France? Does he dare to presume to scorn us in this manner?"

"I told your majesty as much before," Queen Margaret said. "This proves Edward's 'love' and Warwick's 'honesty.'"

The Earl of Warwick said, "King Louis XI, I here protest, in the sight of Heaven and by the hope I have of Heavenly bliss after I am dead that I am blameless in this misdeed of Edward IV's. He is no more my King, for he dishonors me, but he dishonors himself most of all, if he could see his shame.

"Did I forget that because of the House of York my father came to his untimely death?"

The Earl of Warwick's father had fought against the House of Lancaster and had been captured and killed by Lancastrians, but the Earl of Warwick was so angry that he was blaming the Yorkists for his father's death: If the Yorkists had not rebelled against King Henry VI, his father would still be alive.

The Earl of Warwick continued, "Did I let pass the abuse done to my niece?"

Rumor had it that King Edward IV had tried to take the virginity of the Earl of Warwick's niece.

The Earl of Warwick continued, "Did I encircle the head of Edward IV with the regal crown? Did I take from Henry VI his right by birth to be King of England? And am I rewarded at the end with shame? Shame on Edward IV! What I deserve is honor.

"And to repair my honor that I lost for Edward IV, I here renounce him and return to Henry VI.

"My noble Queen, let former grudges pass, and henceforth I am your true servant. I will revenge Edward IV's wrong to Lady Bona, and I will replant Henry on the throne in his former high rank as King of England."

Queen Margaret replied, "Warwick, these words have turned my hate to love, and I forgive and quite forget old faults, and I rejoice that you have become King Henry VI's friend."

The Earl of Warwick said, "I am so much King Henry VI's friend, yes, his unfeigned friend, that, if King Louis XI will agree to furnish us with some few troops of chosen soldiers, I'll undertake to land them on our coast and force the usurper from the throne by war. His newly made marriage will not result in support for him. And as for Clarence, as my letters tell me, he's very likely now to fall away from him and support Henry VI because Edward IV married more for wanton lust than for honor or for the strength and safety of our country."

Lady Bona said to King Louis XI, "Dear brother-in-law, how shall I, Lady Bona, be revenged except but by your help to this distressed Queen?"

Queen Margaret said to King Louis XI, "Renowned Prince, how shall poor Henry VI live, unless you rescue him from foul despair?"

"My quarrel and this English Queen's quarrel with Edward IV are one and the same," Lady Bona said.

"And my quarrel with Edward IV, fair Lady Bona, joins with yours," the Earl of Warwick said.

King Louis XI replied to the Earl of Warwick, "And my quarrel with Edward IV joins with hers, and yours, and Margaret's."

He said to Queen Margaret, "Therefore, at last I am firmly resolved that you shall have aid."

"Let me give humble thanks for all at once," Queen Margaret replied.

King Louis XI said, "So then, England's messenger, return in haste, and tell false Edward IV, your supposed King, that Louis XI of France is sending over 'entertainers' — troops of soldiers — to revel with him and his new bride. You witnessed what has happened here; go and frighten your King with what you have witnessed."

Lady Bona said, "Tell him that in hope he'll become a widower shortly, I'll wear the willow garland for his sake."

A willow garland is a symbol of unrequited love.

Queen Margaret said, "Tell him that I have laid aside my mourning clothing, and I am ready to put on armor."

The Earl of Warwick said, "Tell him from me that he has done me wrong, and therefore I'll uncrown him before long."

He gave the messenger some money and said, "There's your reward. Leave now."

The messenger exited.

King Louis XI said, "But, Warwick, you and Oxford, with five thousand men, shall cross the seas, and bid false Edward IV to a battle, and when the time is right, this noble Queen and Prince shall follow you with a fresh supply of troops. But before you go, resolve for me my doubt: What pledge do we have of your firm loyalty? How can I be certain that you won't again support Edward IV?"

The Earl of Warwick replied, "This shall assure you of my constant loyalty: If our Queen Margaret and this young Prince Edward agree, I'll join my eldest daughter and my joy to him forthwith in holy wedlock bands. Prince Edward and my eldest daughter shall be married."

Queen Margaret said, "Yes, I agree, and I thank you for your proposed offer.

"Son Edward, Warwick's eldest daughter is beautiful and virtuous. Therefore, don't delay, but give your hand to Warwick, and with your hand and your irrevocable faith, vow that only Warwick's daughter shall be yours and unlike Edward IV, you will marry no one else in her place."

Prince Edward said, "Yes, I accept her, for she well deserves it, and here, to pledge my vow, I give you my hand."

He and the Earl of Warwick shook hands.

King Louis XI said, "Why are we delaying now? These soldiers shall be levied, and you, Lord Bourbon, our high Admiral, shall waft them over the English Channel with our royal fleet. I am impatient for Edward IV to fall by war's misfortune because he mocked making a marriage with a lady of France."

Everyone exited except the Earl of Warwick, who said to himself, "I came from Edward IV as an ambassador, but I return as his sworn and mortal foe. To arrange a marriage was the charge he gave to me, but dreadful war shall be the answer to the request he wanted me to make on his behalf.

"Had he no one else to make a dupe but me? Then no one but I shall turn his jest to sorrow. I was the chief person who raised him to the crown, and I'll be the chief person to bring him down again. It's not that I pity Henry VI's misery, but that I seek revenge on Edward's mockery of me."

CHAPTER 4

— 4.1 —

In a room of the palace in London were Duke Richard of Gloucester, Duke George of Clarence, the new Duke of Somerset (son of the Duke of Somerset whom Richard had killed in battle), and the Marquess of Montague.

Duke Richard of Gloucester said sarcastically, "Now tell me, brother Clarence, what do you think of this new marriage of Edward IV with the Lady Elizabeth Grey? Hasn't our brother made a worthy choice?"

"Alas, as you know, it is far from here to France," Duke George of Clarence said sarcastically. "How could he wait until Warwick made his return?"

The Duke of Somerset said, "My lords, don't talk like that; here comes the King."

"And his well-chosen bride," Duke Richard of Gloucester said.

Duke George of Clarence said, "I intend to tell him plainly what I think."

King Edward IV and Lady Elizabeth Grey — who was now Queen Elizabeth, the Queen consort of the King of England — entered the room, along with the Earl of Pembroke, Lord Stafford, Lord Hastings, and others.

A Queen consort is the wife of a King and does not rule. A Queen regnant, such as Queen Elizabeth I of Shakespeare's time, does rule.

King Edward IV said, "Now, brother Clarence, how do you like our choice of a wife? I can see that you stand pensively, thinking deep thoughts, as if you were half malcontent."

Duke George of Clarence replied sarcastically, "I like it as well as do the French King Louis XI and the English Earl of Warwick, who are so weak of courage and so weak in judgment that they'll take no offence at our insult to Lady Bona and to them."

"Suppose they take offence without a cause," King Edward IV said. "They are only Louis XI and Warwick. I am Edward, your King and Warwick's, and I must have my will."

The word "will" meant desire, including sexual desire.

Duke Richard of Gloucester said, "And you shall have your will because you are our King. Yet hasty, impulsive marriages seldom turn out well."

"Brother Richard, are you offended, too?" King Edward IV asked.

"Not I," Duke Richard of Gloucester replied. "No, God forbid that I should wish them severed whom God has joined together. Yes, and it would be a pity to sunder them who yoke so well together."

The word "yoke" meant both joined in marriage and joined in sex.

King Edward IV said, "Setting your scorns and your dislike aside, tell me some reason why Lady Elizabeth Grey should not be my wife and England's Queen. And you, too, Somerset and Montague, speak freely what you think."

Duke George of Clarence said, "Then this is my opinion: King Louis XI of France will become your enemy because you have mocked him by asking for marriage with the Lady Bona but marrying someone else."

Duke Richard of Gloucester said, "And Warwick, by doing what you ordered him to do, is now dishonored by this new marriage of yours."

King Edward IV replied, "What if both Louis XI and Warwick should be appeased by some scheme that I devise?"

The Marquess of Montague said, "Still, to have joined with France in an alliance would have strengthened this our commonwealth more against foreign storms than any home-bred marriage. By marrying Lady Elizabeth Grey, you have dashed the hope of an alliance by marriage with the King of France."

Lord Hastings said, "Why, doesn't Montague know that of itself England is safe, if true within itself?"

The Marquess of Montague said, "But England is safer when it is allied with France."

Lord Hastings said, "It is better to use France than to trust France. Let us be allied with God and with the seas that He has given us to serve as an impregnable fence. Using only God's and the seas' help, we can defend ourselves: In God and the seas and in ourselves our safety lies."

Duke George of Clarence said, "For this one speech Lord Hastings well deserves to have the heir of the Lord Hungerford as a wife."

King Edward IV said, "Yes, and what of that? It was my will and grant, and for this once my will shall stand for law."

Duke Richard of Gloucester said, "And yet I think your grace has not done well to give the heir and daughter of Lord Scales to the brother of your loving bride. She would have better fitted Clarence or me. But in your bride you bury brotherhood."

Duke George of Clarence said, "Or else you would not have bestowed the heir of the Lord Bonville on your new wife's son and left your brothers to go and find prosperity elsewhere."

King Edward IV had been raising the status and wealth of Queen Elizabeth's male relatives by arranging good marriages to wealthy women for them.

"Alas, poor Clarence!" King Edward IV said sarcastically. "Is it for a wife that you are malcontent? I will provide a wife for you."

Duke George of Clarence replied, "In choosing for yourself, you showed your judgment, which was shallow; therefore, give me permission to play the marriage broker in my own behalf, and to that end — the end of getting a wife — I intend to leave you shortly."

King Edward IV said, "Whether you leave or stay, I, Edward, will be King, and not be bound by his brother's will."

Queen Elizabeth now spoke up: "My lords, before it pleased his majesty to raise my state to the title of a Queen, you must all confess — if you do me right — that I was not ignoble of descent and that women of lower rank than I have had like fortune.

"But as this title honors me and mine, so your dislike of my marriage, dislike by those whom I would like to please, clouds my joys with danger and with sorrow."

King Edward IV said to her, "My love, don't fawn upon their frowns. What danger or what sorrow can befall you as long as Edward is your constant friend and their true sovereign, whom they must obey?

"They shall obey, and they shall love you, too, unless they seek for hatred at my hands, which if they do, I will still keep you safe, and they shall feel the vengeance of my wrath."

Duke Richard of Gloucester thought, *I hear, yet I don't say much, but I think much more.*

The messenger who had gone to France with letters for the King of France, the Earl of Warwick, and Queen Margaret entered the room.

King Edward IV recognized him and asked, "Now, messenger, what letters or what news do you have from France?"

The messenger replied, "My sovereign liege, no letters, and few words, but such words as I, without your special pardon, dare not tell you."

King Edward IV said, "Go on, for we pardon you; therefore, briefly tell me their words as accurately as you can remember them. What answer does King Louis XI make to our letter?"

"At my departure, he said these very words, 'Tell false Edward IV, your supposed King, that Louis XI of France is sending over 'entertainers' — troops of soldiers — to revel with him and his new bride.'"

"Is Louis XI so daring?" King Edward IV said. "Perhaps he thinks that I am Henry VI.

"But what did Lady Bona say about my marriage to Lady Elizabeth Grey?"

The messenger replied, "These were her words, uttered with mad disdain: 'Tell him, in hope he'll prove a widower shortly, I'll wear the willow garland for his sake.'"

"I don't blame her," King Edward IV said. "She could say little less; she had wrong done to her.

"But what did Henry VI's Queen Margaret say? For I have heard that she was there in person."

The messenger replied, "She said, 'Tell him that I have laid aside my mourning clothing, and I am ready to put on armor.'"

"Perhaps she intends to play the role of an Amazonian woman-warrior," King Edward IV said. "But what did the Earl of Warwick say concerning these insults?"

The messenger replied, "He, more incensed against your majesty than all the rest, discharged me with these words: 'Tell him from me that he has done me wrong, and therefore I'll uncrown him before long.'"

"Ha!" King Edward IV said. "Does the traitor dare breathe out such proud words?

"Well, I will arm myself, being thus forewarned. They shall have wars and pay for their presumption.

"But tell me, is Warwick friends with Queen Margaret?"

"Yes, gracious sovereign," the messenger replied. "They are so linked in friendship that young Prince Edward will marry Warwick's daughter."

Duke George of Clarence said, "He will probably marry Warwick's elder daughter. I, Clarence, will have and marry Warwick's younger daughter.

"Now, brother King, farewell, and sit yourself firmly on the throne, for I will go from here to Warwick's other daughter, so that, although I lack a Kingdom, yet in marriage I may not prove to be inferior to yourself.

"Anyone who loves and respects me and Warwick, follow me."

Duke George of Clarence and the Duke of Somerset exited.

Duke Richard of Gloucester thought, *Not I; I won't exit. My thoughts aim at a further matter; I stay not because of love for Edward, but because of love for the crown.*

King Edward IV said, "Both the Duke of Clarence and the Duke of Somerset have gone to join Warwick! Yet I am armed against the worst that can happen, and haste is necessary in this desperate case.

"Lord Pembroke and Lord Stafford, you two go and levy men in our behalf, and make preparations for war. The enemy soldiers are already or quickly will be landed. I myself in person will immediately follow you."

The Earl of Pembroke and Lord Stafford exited.

King Edward IV continued, "But, before I go, Lord Hastings and the Marquess of Montague, resolve and remove my doubt. You two, of all the rest, are close to Warwick by blood and by alliance. Tell me whether you love and respect Warwick more than me. If you do, then both of you depart and go to him. I would rather wish you to be my foes than to be my hollow, insincere friends. But if you intend to hold and maintain your true obedience to me, your lawful King, give me assurance with some friendly vow, so that I may never be suspicious of you."

"May God help Montague only to the extent that he proves true and loyal to you!" the Marquess of Montague said.

"And may God help Hastings only to the extent that he favors Edward's cause!" Lord Hastings said.

King Edward IV then said, "Now, brother Richard, will you stand by us?"

Duke Richard of Gloucester said, "Yes, in defiance of all who shall stand against you."

"Why, good!" King Edward IV said. "Then I am sure of victory. Now therefore let us go from here, and waste no hour, until we meet Warwick with his foreign power."

The Earl of Warwick and the Earl of Oxford talked together on a plain in Warwickshire. French soldiers were also present.

The Earl of Warwick said, "Trust me, my lord, everything has gone well up to now. The common people in great numbers swarm to us."

Duke George of Clarence and the Duke of Somerset arrived.

The Earl of Warwick continued, "But see where Somerset and Clarence come!

"Tell me quickly, my lords, are we all friends?"

Duke George of Clarence replied, "Don't be afraid that we are not your friends, my lord, for I assure you that we are."

The Earl of Warwick said, "Then, gentle Clarence, Warwick welcomes you, and welcome to you, Somerset. I regard it as cowardice to remain mistrustful where a noble heart has pledged an open hand in sign of love and friendship. Otherwise I might think that Clarence, Edward IV's brother, were only a feigned friend to our proceedings.

"But welcome, sweet Clarence; my daughter shall be yours. And now, because your brother Edward IV is carelessly encamped, his soldiers are idling in the nearby towns, and he is attended only by a minimal guard, what remains to be done but under the cover of night, we ambush and capture him at our pleasure?

"Our scouts have determined that the venture will be very easy to accomplish. Just as Ulysses and brave Diomedes with cunning and manliness stole to King Rhesus' tents, and brought away the Thracian steeds of fate, so we, well covered with the night's black mantle, without warning may beat down Edward IV's guard and seize the King himself."

During the Trojan War, the Greeks Ulysses and Diomedes made a night raid on King Rhesus of Thrace and slaughtered him and many of his men and captured his horses and drove them back to the Greek camp. Some sources state that the raid was made because of a prophecy that if the horses grazed on the grass and drank from a river at Troy, then Troy would never fall, and so Ulysses and Diomedes made the raid before the Thracian horses could graze on Trojan grass and drink Trojan water.

The Earl of Warwick continued, "I say that we will not slaughter him, for I intend only to surprise and capture him.

"You who will follow me in this attempt, applaud the name of Henry VI with your leader."

They all cried, "Henry!"

The Earl of Warwick continued, "Why, then, let's go on our way silently. We fight for Warwick and his friends, for God, and for Saint George!"

Three watchmen who were assigned to guard King Edward IV's tent talked together outside the tent.

The first watchman said, "Come on, my masters; each man take his stand. The King by this time has set himself down in a chair to sleep."

"Won't he go to bed?" the second watchman said.

"Why, no," the first watchman replied, "for he has made a solemn vow never to lie and take his natural rest until either Warwick or himself is quite suppressed."

The second watchman said, "Tomorrow then shall likely be the day we see who is suppressed if Warwick is as near as men report he is."

The third watchman said, "But tell me, please, which nobleman is that who with the King here rests in his tent?"

"He is the Lord Hastings, the King's chiefest friend," the first watchman replied.

"Oh, is that him?" the third watchman said. "But why does the King command that his chief followers lodge in nearby towns, while the King himself lodges in the cold field?"

"It is more honorable," the second watchman said, "because it is more dangerous."

The third watchman said, "Yes, but give me dignified ease, comfortable dignity, and quietness. I like those things better than a dangerous honor. If Warwick knew in what circumstances King Edward IV is lodging, I fear that Warwick would awaken the King."

"Unless our halberds prevented his attempt to go to and awaken King Edward IV," the first watchman said.

"Yes," the second watchman said. "Why else do we guard King Edward IV's royal tent but to defend his person from night-foes?"

The Earl of Warwick, Duke George of Clarence, the Earl of Oxford, the Duke of Somerset, and some French soldiers silently crept up on the watchmen.

"This is his tent," the Earl of Warwick said quietly. "See where stand his guards. Courage, my masters! Acquire honor now or never! Just follow me, and Edward IV shall be ours."

The first watchman asked, "Who goes there?"

"Stop, or you die!" the second watchman said.

The Earl of Warwick and the others with him all cried, "Warwick! Warwick!" and set upon the watchmen, who fled, crying "Arm! Arm!" The Earl of Warwick and the others pursued them.

The cry "Arm!" meant, "Supporters of King Edward IV, arm yourselves! Get your weapons!"

In the turmoil, Duke Richard of Gloucester and Lord Hastings fled.

Soon, the Earl of Warwick and the others with him captured King Edward IV.

The Duke of Somerset asked, "Who were the men who fled?"

The Earl of Warwick replied, "They were Richard and Hastings, but let them go. Here we have captured the Duke of York."

"'The Duke of York!'" King Edward IV said. "Why, Warwick, when we parted, you called me King."

"Yes, but the case is altered," the Earl of Warwick replied. "When you disgraced me in my embassy to the French King, then I degraded you from being the English King, and I have come now to make you Duke of York. Too bad! How could you govern any Kingdom, you who do not know how to treat ambassadors, and do not know how to be contented with one wife, and do not know how to treat your brothers brotherly, and do not know how to take pains for the people's welfare, and do not know how to shroud yourself from enemies?"

King Edward IV said, "Brother of Clarence, are you here, too? Then I see that Edward IV must necessarily fall as King.

"Yet, Warwick, in defiance of all misfortune, and in defiance of you yourself and all your accomplices, Edward will always bear himself as King of England. Although the malice of Lady Fortune overthrows my Kingship, my mind exceeds the compass of her Wheel of Fortune that lowers and raises men."

"Then, let Edward be England's King, but only in his own mind," the Earl of Warwick said.

He took off Edward IV's crown and said, "But Henry VI now shall wear the English crown, and be the true King of England indeed, while you are only the shadow of a King.

"My Lord of Somerset, at my request, see that Duke Edward of York is immediately conveyed to my brother: the Archbishop of York. After I have fought a battle against the Earl of Pembroke and his soldiers, I'll follow you and tell what answer King Louis XI and the Lady Bona have sent to Duke Edward of York.

"Now, for a while farewell, good Duke Edward of York."

King Edward IV said, "What the Fates, goddesses of destiny, impose, men must necessarily abide; it is useless to resist both wind and tide."

Soldiers forcibly led away Duke Edward of York.

The Earl of Oxford asked, "What now remains, my lords, for us to do but march to London with our soldiers?"

The Earl of Warwick replied, "Yes, that's the first thing that we have to do: We need to free King Henry VI from imprisonment and see him seated on the regal throne."

<h1 style="text-align:center">— 4.4 —</h1>

Queen Elizabeth and her brother Earl Rivers talked together in a room in the palace in London.

Earl Rivers asked, "Madam, what is the reason for this sudden change?"

Queen Elizabeth replied, "Why, brother Rivers, are you yet to learn what recent misfortune has befallen King Edward IV?"

"Is it the loss of some pitched battle against Warwick?" Earl Rivers asked.

"No," Queen Elizabeth replied. "It is the loss of his own royal person."

"Then is my sovereign slain?" Earl Rivers asked.

"Yes, he is almost slain, for he has been taken prisoner," Queen Elizabeth replied. "He was either betrayed by the treachery of his guards or was surprised and captured without warning by his foe, and as I understand further, he has been recently committed to the custody of the Archbishop of York, who is cruel Warwick's brother and therefore our foe."

"This news I must confess is full of grief, gracious madam," Earl Rivers said, "yet bear it as you may. Warwick may lose, although for now he has won the day."

"Until then fair hope must hinder life's decay," Queen Elizabeth replied. "And I would rather wean myself from despair because of my love for Edward IV's offspring in my womb. My pregnancy is what makes me bridle passion and bear with mildness the cross of my misfortune. Yes, yes, because of my pregnancy I draw in many a tear and stop the rising of health-destroying sighs, lest with my sighs or tears I blight or drown King Edward IV's fruit, the true heir to the English crown."

"But, madam, what has become of Warwick?" Earl Rivers asked.

"I am informed that he is coming towards London in order to set the crown once more on Henry VI's head," Queen Elizabeth replied. "You can guess the rest. King Edward IV's friends must fall, but to prevent the tyrant Warwick's violence — for we ought not to trust a man who has once broken his vow — I'll go immediately away from here and to the sanctuary, to save at least the heir of Edward's rightful claim to the crown of England. There I shall rest secure and safe from force and fraud. Come, therefore, let us flee while we may flee. If Warwick should capture us, we are sure to die."

Duke Richard of Gloucester, Lord Hastings, and Sir William Stanley talked together in a park — a hunting ground — near Middleham Castle in Yorkshire. Some soldiers were with them. The Archbishop of York owned the park.

Duke Richard of Gloucester said, "Now, my Lord Hastings and Sir William Stanley, stop wondering why I drew you hither into this most densely wooded thicket of the park. Thus stands the case: You know our King, my brother, is prisoner to the Archbishop of York here, at whose hands he has received good treatment and great liberty, and, often attended only by a weak guard, he comes hunting in this area to entertain himself. I have informed him by secret means that if about this hour he would make his way here under the pretense of his usual entertainment, he shall here find his friends with horses and men to set him free from his captivity."

King Edward IV and a huntsman arrived.

The huntsman said, "This way, my lord, for this way lies the quarry."

King Edward IV replied, "No, this way, man. See where the huntsmen stand."

Duke Richard of Gloucester, Lord Hastings, Sir William Stanley, and the soldiers showed themselves. King Edward IV's guard, the huntsman, was outnumbered and unable to resist.

King Edward IV said, "Now, brother of Gloucester, Lord Hastings, and the rest, do you stand thus close in order to steal the Archbishop's 'deer'?"

Duke Richard of Gloucester replied, "Brother, the time and case require haste. Your horse stands ready at the corner of the park."

"But whither shall we go afterward?" King Edward IV asked.

"To Lynn, my lord," Lord Hastings replied, "and ship from thence to Flanders."

"Well guessed, believe me," Duke Richard of Gloucester said, "for that was my intention."

King Edward IV said, "Sir William Stanley, I will reward your zeal."

Duke Richard of Gloucester said, "But why do we stay here? This is no time to talk."

King Edward IV said, "Huntsman, what do you say? Will you come along with us?"

The huntsman replied, "It is better to do that than to tarry here and be hanged."

"Come then, let's go," Duke Richard of Gloucester said. "Let's have no more ado."

"Archbishop, farewell," King Edward IV said, facing the direction of the Archbishop's home. "May God shield you from Warwick's frown, and may you pray that I repossess the crown."

In a room of the Tower of London, many people stood: King Henry VI, Duke George of Clarence, the Earl of Warwick, the Duke of Somerset, Earl Henry of Richmond, the Earl of Oxford, the Marquess of Montague, and the Lieutenant of the Tower. The Marquess of Montague now supported King Henry VI and the Earl of Warwick.

King Henry VI said, "Master Lieutenant, now that God and friends have shaken Edward from the regal seat, and turned my captive state to liberty, my fear to hope, my sorrows to joys, what are the fees I owe you now that I am free?"

Wealthy prisoners paid for their food and keep after being released from prison. Of course, King Henry VI, if he were a different kind of person, could have the Lieutenant of the Tower executed.

The Lieutenant of the Tower replied, "Subjects may demand as a right nothing from their sovereigns, but if a humble person who prays to you may prevail, then I crave the pardon of your majesty."

"Pardon for what, Lieutenant?" King Henry VI said. "For treating me well? You can be sure I'll well repay your kindness because it made my imprisonment a pleasure. Yes, such a pleasure as caged birds feel when after many melancholy thoughts, they at last because of the harmonic sounds of the household quite forget their loss of liberty.

"But, Warwick, after God, you are responsible for setting me free, and chiefly therefore I thank God and you. God was the author and instigator; you were the instrument and agent of His plan.

"Therefore, so that I may conquer Lady Fortune's spite by living low on the Wheel of Fortune, where Lady Fortune cannot hurt me, and so that the people of this blessed land may not be punished with my perverse stars that bring misfortune, Warwick, although my head shall still wear the crown, I here resign my government to you, for you are fortunate in all your deeds while I am unfortunate in all my deeds."

The Earl of Warwick replied, "Your grace has always been famed for being virtuous, and now you may be seen to be as wise as virtuous because you have spied on and avoided Lady Fortune's malice, for few men rightly conform their temperament with the stars. Few men can rightly react to what the stars bring them. Yet in this one thing let me blame your grace: for choosing me when Clarence is present and available."

Duke George of Clarence said, "No, Warwick, you are worthy of the position of authority. To you the Heavens in your nativity gave an olive branch and a laurel crown because you were likely to be blest both in peace and in war, and therefore I give you my free consent for you to hold this high office."

The Earl of Warwick replied, "And I choose only Clarence for Lord Protector."

King Henry VI said, "Warwick and Clarence, both of you give me your hands. Now join your hands, and with your hands your hearts, so that no dissension may hinder government and the proper exercise of authority over Britain. I make you both Lord Protectors of this land, while I myself will lead a private life and spend my final days in devotion to rebuke sin and to praise my Creator."

"What does Clarence answer to his sovereign's will?" the Earl of Warwick asked.

Duke George of Clarence replied, "He answers that he consents, if Warwick will also yield his consent, for on your fortune I myself happily rely."

The Earl of Warwick said, "Why, then, although I am loath to wield this power, yet I must be content. We'll yoke together, like a double shadow to Henry's body, and occupy his place as his substitutes — I mean, in bearing the weight of government and certainly not as usurpers — while he enjoys the honor of being King and enjoys his ease.

"And, Clarence, it is more than necessary that immediately Edward IV be pronounced a traitor, and all his lands and goods be confiscated."

"Of course. What else?" Duke George of Clarence replied. "And it is necessary that the succession be determined."

The Earl of Warwick said, "Yes, and therein Clarence shall not lack his part."

When Henry VI died, his son was next in time to be King. But if both Henry VI and Prince Edward died before Prince Edward had children, then Duke George of Clarence would be next in line to be King because Edward IV was a traitor.

King Henry VI said, "But, with the first of all your chief affairs, let me entreat you, for I no longer command you, that Margaret your Queen and my son, Prince Edward, be sent for to return from France quickly because until I see them here my joy in my liberty is half eclipsed by disquieting fear and dread."

Duke George of Clarence replied, "It shall be done, my sovereign, with all speed possible."

Seeing a young man nearby, King Henry VI asked, "My Lord of Somerset, what youth is that, of whom you seem to take so tender care?"

The Duke of Somerset replied, "My liege, it is young Henry, Earl of Richmond."

King Henry VI said, "Come hither, England's hope."

In a traditional gesture of prophecy, King Henry VI laid his hand on the head of the young Henry, Earl of Richmond.

King Henry VI said, "If secret powers suggest the truth to my divining and future-foretelling thoughts, this pretty lad will prove to be our country's bliss. His looks are full of peaceful majesty, his head by nature framed to wear a crown, his hand to wield a scepter, and himself likely in time to bless a regal throne. Make much of him, my lords, for this is the one who must help you more than you are hurt by me."

Young Henry, Earl of Richmond, would become King Henry VII. He would end the Wars of the Roses and begin the Tudor Dynasty.

A messenger arrived.

The Earl of Warwick asked, "What is your news, my friend?"

The messenger replied, "That Edward IV has escaped from your brother, and fled, as your brother has heard since, to Burgundy."

"This is unsavory news!" the Earl of Warwick said. "But how did he make his escape?"

The messenger replied, "He was conveyed away by Duke Richard of Gloucester and Lord Hastings, who waited for him in secret ambush at the side of the forest and rescued him from the Archbishop's huntsmen, for hunting was Edward IV's daily exercise."

The Earl of Warwick said, "My brother was too careless of his charge. He was too careless in doing his duty. But let us go from here, my sovereign, in order that we may provide a salve for any sore that may happen."

Everyone exited except the Duke of Somerset, young Earl Henry of Richmond, and the Earl of Oxford.

The Duke of Somerset said to the Earl of Oxford, "My lord, I don't like this flight of Edward IV's, for doubtless the Duke of Burgundy will give him help, and we shall have more wars before long. As Henry VI's recent presaging prophecy gladdened my heart with hope concerning this young Earl Henry of Richmond, so does my heart make me apprehensive about what may happen to him in these conflicts, to his harm and ours. Therefore, Lord Oxford, to prevent the worst, immediately we'll send him hence to Brittany, until the storms of civil enmity have passed."

"Yes," the Earl of Oxford said, "for if Edward IV repossesses the crown, it is likely that young Earl Henry of Richmond along with the rest shall fall."

The Duke of Somerset said, "It shall be so; the young Earl Henry of Richmond shall go to Brittany. Come, therefore, let's set about doing it speedily."

— 4.7 —

Before the town of York stood King Edward IV, Duke Richard of Gloucester, Lord Hastings, and some soldiers.

King Edward IV said, "Now, brother Richard, Lord Hastings, and the rest, so far Lady Fortune is making us amends and says that once more I shall exchange my diminished state for Henry VI's regal crown. Well have we passed and now again passed the seas and brought desired help from Burgundy. What then remains, we being thus arrived from Ravenspurgh Haven before the gates of York, but that we enter York, as into our Dukedom? I am, after all, the Duke of York."

Duke Richard of Gloucester said, "The gates are firmly bolted against us! Brother, I don't like this, for many men who stumble at the threshold are well given notice that danger lurks within."

Superstition held that stumbling at the threshold was an omen of bad luck.

King Edward IV said, "Tush, man. Omens must not now frighten us. By fair or foul means, we must enter York, for here our friends will come to join us."

Lord Hastings said, "My liege, I'll knock once more to summon them."

He knocked, and on the city walls appeared the Mayor of York and the Aldermen of York.

The Mayor of York said, "My lords, we were forewarned of your coming, and we shut the gates for our own safety because now we owe allegiance to King Henry VI."

King Edward IV said, "But, master Mayor, if Henry VI is your King, Edward at the least is still the Duke of York."

"That is true, my good lord," the Mayor of York said. "I know you to be no less."

King Edward IV said, "Why, I demand nothing but my Dukedom, for I am well content with that alone."

Duke Richard of Gloucester said quietly, "But when the fox has once got in his nose, it'll soon find a way to make the body follow."

Lord Hastings said, "Master Mayor, why do you stand there and doubt what you hear? Open the gates; we are King Henry VI's friends."

The Mayor of York said, "Do you say so? The gates shall then be opened."

The Mayor of York and the Aldermen of York descended from the walls in order to open the gates.

Duke Richard of Gloucester said sarcastically, "He is a wise and brave Captain, and soon persuaded!"

Lord Hastings said, "The good old man would fain that all were well, so it were not 'long of him."

This meant both 1) "The good old man would like that all were well, so long as all being well — opening the gates — were not along — associated — with him," and 2) "The good old man would like that all were well, so long as all being well — opening the gates — would not belong to him."

In other words, "The good old man would like that all were well, so long as the blame for opening the gates was not his."

Lord Hastings continued, "But once we pass through the gates and enter the city, I don't doubt that we shall soon persuade both him and all his brothers, aka the Aldermen, to see reason — to see that Edward IV is King of England."

The Mayor and the two Aldermen opened the gates and came out of the city.

King Edward IV said, "So, master Mayor, these gates must not be shut except in the nighttime or in the time of war. Don't be afraid, man, but give me the keys to the gates."

He took the keys and added, "For I, Edward, will defend the town and you, and all those friends who deign to follow me."

The sound of a military drummer was heard and Sir John Montgomery arrived along with the drummer and some soldiers.

Duke Richard of Gloucester said, "Brother, this is Sir John Montgomery, our trusty friend, unless I am deceived."

King Edward IV said, "Welcome, Sir John! But why have you come in arms?"

Sir John Montgomery replied, "To help King Edward IV in his time of storm, as every loyal subject ought to do."

"Thanks, good Montgomery," King Edward IV said, "but we now forget our title to the crown and we claim only our Dukedom until God is pleased to send the rest."

"Then fare you well, for I will go away from here again," Sir John Montgomery said. "I came to serve a King and not a Duke.

"Drummer, strike up, and let us march away."

"No, Sir John," King Edward IV said. "Stay awhile, and we'll debate and discuss by what safe means the crown may be recovered."

"Why do you talk of debating?" Sir John Montgomery said. "In few words, I say to you that if you'll not here proclaim yourself our King, I'll leave you to your fortune and leave to keep back anyone who comes to succor you. Why shall we fight, if you claim no title of Kingship?"

Duke Richard of Gloucester said to Edward IV, "Why, brother, do you dwell on trivial details?"

King Edward IV said, "When we grow stronger, then we'll make our claim. Until then, it is wise to conceal our intentions."

"Away with scrupulous wit!" Lord Hastings said. "Now arms must rule."

"And fearless minds climb soonest to crowns," Duke Richard of Gloucester said. "Brother, we will proclaim you King immediately. The report of this will bring you many friends."

"Then be it as you will," King Edward IV said, "for it is my right, and Henry VI only usurps the diadem."

Sir John Montgomery said, "Yes, now my sovereign speaks like himself, and now I will be Edward IV's champion and defender."

Lord Hastings ordered, "Blow, trumpeter. Edward shall be here proclaimed King.

"Come, fellow-soldier, you make the proclamation."

The trumpet sounded, and the soldier read, "*Edward IV, by the grace of God, King of England and France, and lord of Ireland, and etc.*"

Sir John Montgomery said, "And whosoever denies Edward IV's right to be King of England, by this I challenge him to single combat."

He threw down his gauntlet.

Everyone shouted, "Long live Edward IV!"

King Edward IV said, "Thanks, brave Montgomery, and thanks to you all. If Lady Fortune serves me well, I'll repay this kindness.

"Now, for this night, let's harbor and lodge here in York, and when the morning Sun shall raise his chariot above the border of this horizon and dawn arrives, we'll go forward to meet Warwick and his mates, for I know well that Henry VI is no soldier.

"Ah, perverse, obstinate Clarence! How evil it is for you to flatter Henry and forsake your brother! Yet, as we may, we'll meet both you and Warwick.

"Come on, brave soldiers. Don't doubt that we will win the day, and, don't doubt that you will receive large pay once the day is won."

A number of people met in a room in the Bishop's Palace in London: King Henry VI, the Earl of Warwick, the Marquess of Montague, Duke George of Clarence, the Duke of Exeter, and the Earl of Oxford.

"What advice can you give, my lords?" the Earl of Warwick said. "Edward from Flanders in Belgium, with rash Germans and rough, uncivilized Hollanders, has passed in safety through the narrow seas, and with his troops he marches at full speed to London, and many inconstant, fickle people flock to him."

"Let's levy men, and beat him back again," King Henry VI said.

Duke George of Clarence said, "A little fire is quickly trodden out, but if the fire is allowed to grow, rivers cannot quench it."

The Earl of Warwick said, "In Warwickshire I have true-hearted friends who are not mutinous in peace yet are bold in war. Those I will muster up.

"You, my son-in-law Clarence, shall stir the knights and gentlemen in Suffolk, Norfolk, and Kent to come with you.

"You, brother Marquess of Montague, in Buckingham, Northampton, and Leicestershire shall find men well inclined to hear what you command.

"And you, brave Oxford, who is wondrously well beloved in Oxfordshire, shall muster up your friends.

"My sovereign, King Henry VI, with the loving citizens, like his island girdled by the ocean, or like modest, chaste Diana encircled by her nymphs, shall rest in London until we come to him.

"Fair lords, take leave and do not delay in order to reply.

"Farewell, my sovereign."

"Farewell, my Hector, and my Troy's true hope," King Henry VI said.

Hector was the foremost warrior for Troy during the Trojan War. London was thought of as *Troia Nova*, or New Troy, because a grandson of Aeneas, another important Trojan warrior, was believed to have founded it.

Kissing Henry VI's hand, Duke George of Clarence said, "In sign of my truth and loyalty to you, I kiss your highness' hand."

King Henry VI replied, "Well-minded, loyal Clarence, may you be favored by Lady Fortune!"

The Marquess of Montague said, "Take comfort, my lord, and so I take my leave."

"And thus I seal my truth, and bid adieu to you," the Earl of Oxford said.

"Sweet Oxford, and my loving Montague, and everyone all at once, once more I say to you a happy farewell," King Henry VI said.

"Farewell, sweet lords," the Earl of Warwick said. "Let's meet at Coventry."

Everyone exited except King Henry VI and the Duke of Exeter.

"Here at the palace I will rest awhile," King Henry VI said. "Cousin of Exeter, what does your lordship think? I think the army that Edward IV has in the field should not be able to oppose and defeat mine."

"The fear is that he will persuade others to desert their allegiance to you," the Duke of Exeter said.

"That's not my fear," King Henry VI said. "My merit has gotten me a good reputation. I have not stopped my ears so I can't hear my subjects' requests, nor have I put off their petitions with slow delays. My pity has been balm to heal their wounds. My mildness has allayed their swelling griefs. My mercy has dried their water-flowing tears. I have not been desirous of their wealth, nor have I much oppressed them with great taxation. Nor am I eager for or inclined to revenge, although my subjects have much erred. So why then should they love Edward more than me?

"No, Exeter, these virtues of mine lay claim to my subjects' goodwill. And when the lion fawns upon the lamb, the lamb will never cease to follow him."

Shouts were heard from outside: "Protect Lancaster! Protect Lancaster!"

The Duke of Exeter said, "Listen! Listen, my lord! What shouts are these?"

The shouts were due to King Edward IV's Yorkist soldiers attacking the palace in order to capture the Lancastrian King Henry VI.

King Edward IV, Duke Richard of Gloucester, and some Yorkist soldiers entered the room.

King Edward IV said, "Seize the shy, retiring Henry VI and carry him away from here, and once again proclaim us King of England.

"You, Henry VI, are the spring that makes small brooks flow. Now your spring stops; my sea shall suck your brooks dry and swell so much the higher by their ebb.

"Take Henry VI to the Tower of London; don't let him speak.

"And, lords, we will bend our course towards Coventry, where peremptory Warwick now remains.

"The sun shines hot, and if we delay, cold biting winter will mar our hoped-for hay."

Duke Richard of Gloucester said, "Let's leave at once, before the Earl of Warwick's forces join, and let's take the greatly grown traitor unawares.

"Brave warriors, march at full speed towards Coventry."

CHAPTER 5

— 5.1 —

The Earl of Warwick, the Mayor of Coventry, two messengers, and some others stood upon the walls of Coventry.

The Earl of Warwick asked, "Where is the messenger who came from the valiant Earl of Oxford? How far away is your lord, my honest fellow?"

The first messenger replied, "By this time, he is at Dunsmore, marching to here."

The Earl of Warwick then asked, "How far away is our brother the Marquess of Montague? Where is the messenger who came from Montague?"

The second messenger replied, "By this time, he is at Daintry, with a powerful troop of soldiers."

Sir John Somerville arrived.

The Earl of Warwick asked, "Tell me, Somerville, what says my loving son-in-law? And, by your guess, how near is Duke George of Clarence now?"

Sir John Somerville replied, "At Southam I left Duke George of Clarence with his forces, and I expect him to be here some two hours from now."

They heard the sound of a drum.

The Earl of Warwick said, "Clarence is at hand. I hear his drum."

"It is not his, my lord," Sir John Somerville said. He pointed and said, "In this direction Southam lies. The drum your honor hears is marching from Warwick."

The Earl of Warwick said, "Who would they be? Probably, unlooked-for friends."

Sir John Somerville said, "They are at hand, and you shall quickly know who they are."

King Edward IV, Duke Richard of Gloucester, and many soldiers arrived.

King Edward IV ordered, "Go, trumpeter, to the walls, and sound a parley."

Duke Richard of Gloucester said, "See how the surly Warwick mans the wall!"

The Earl of Warwick said, "Oh, unbidden, spiteful annoyance! Has lascivious Edward IV come? Where did our scouts sleep, or how were they seduced, that we could hear no news of Edward IV's coming here?"

King Edward IV said, "Now, Warwick, will you open the city gates, speak gentle words and humbly bend your knee, call me your King, and at my hands beg mercy? If you do, we shall pardon you these outrages."

"No," the Earl of Warwick said. "Rather, will you withdraw your forces from here, confess who set you up and plucked you down, call Warwick your patron, and be penitent? If you do, you shall continue to be the Duke of York."

Duke Richard of Gloucester joked, "I thought, at least, he would have said, 'You shall continue to be the King,' or is he jesting against his will?"

"Is not a Dukedom, sir, a goodly gift?" the Earl of Warwick asked.

Duke Richard of Gloucester replied, "Yes, by my faith, for a poor Earl to give."

Dukes outrank Earls.

Duke Richard of Gloucester continued, sarcastically, "I'll serve you for so good a gift."

The Earl of Warwick said, "It was I who gave the Kingdom to your brother."

"Why, then it is mine, if only by Warwick's gift," King Edward IV said.

"You are no Atlas for so great a weight," the Earl of Warwick said.

Atlas is the mythological Titan who holds up the sky on his shoulders.

The Earl of Warwick continued, "And, you weakling, Warwick takes his gift back again. Henry VI is my King, and Warwick is his subject."

King Edward IV said, "But Warwick's King Henry VI is Edward IV's prisoner. And, gallant Warwick, just answer this: What is the body when the head is off?"

"It's a pity that Warwick had no more foresight," Duke Richard of Gloucester said. "While he thought to steal the poor, feeble ten, the King was slyly stolen from the deck of cards!"

A ten is not a court card; court cards are the Jack, Queen, and King. Duke Richard of Gloucester was saying that when the Earl of Warwick was rescuing Henry VI from captivity, he was not rescuing a legitimate member of the royal court.

He continued, "You left poor Henry VI at the Bishop's Palace, and, ten to one, you'll meet him in the Tower of London."

"All this is true," King Edward IV said, "yet you are still the same old Warwick. This news will not change your opposition to me."

Duke Richard of Gloucester said, "Come, Warwick, adjust yourself to the time; kneel down, kneel down. No? If not now, when? Strike now, or else the iron cools."

"Strike" could mean 1) Strike a blow, or 2) Strike — lower — your topsail in deference or in surrender. Richard wanted Warwick to take action quickly.

The Earl of Warwick raised his hand and replied, "I would rather chop this hand off at a blow, and with the other hand fling it at your face, than bear so low a sail as to strike and lower my topsail to you."

King Edward IV raised his hand and said, "Sail however you can, have wind and tide as your friends, this hand, fast wound about your coal-black hair shall, while your head is warm and newly cut off, write in the dust this sentence with your blood, 'Changing-with-the-wind Warwick now can change sides no more.'"

The Earl of Oxford arrived with a drummer and his colors — his battle flags — and his army.

The Earl of Warwick said, "Oh, cheerful colors! Oh, cheerful battle flags! See where Oxford is coming!"

The Earl of Oxford cried, "Oxford, Oxford, for the House of Lancaster!"

He and his army entered the city of Coventry.

Duke Richard of Gloucester said, "The gates are open; let us enter, too."

King Edward IV replied, "If we do that, other foes may attack our backs. Instead, we will stand here in good array, for they no doubt will issue out again and challenge us to battle them. If they don't, since the city has only a weak defense, we'll quickly rouse the traitors out of their den."

The Earl of Warwick said, "You are welcome, Oxford, for we need your help."

The Marquess of Montague arrived with his troops, drummer, and battle flags.

He cried, "Montague, Montague, for the House of Lancaster!"

He and his troops entered the city.

Duke Richard of Gloucester said, "You and your brother both shall pay for this treason even with the dearest blood your bodies bear."

King Edward IV said, "The more powerful the enemies, the greater the victory. My mind foretells happy gain and conquest."

The Duke of Somerset arrived with his troops, drummer, and battle flags.

He cried, "Somerset, Somerset, for the House of Lancaster!"

He and his troops entered the city.

Duke Richard of Gloucester said, "Two of your name, both of them Dukes of Somerset, have lost their lives to the House of York, and you shall be the third if my sword continues to hold its edge."

Duke George of Clarence arrived with his troops, drummer, and battle flags.

The Earl of Warwick said, "Look where George of Clarence sweeps along with forces enough to challenge his brother to battle; with George of Clarence, an upright zeal for justice prevails more than the nature of a brother's love!"

Duke George of Clarence said, "Clarence for the House of Lancaster!"

King Edward IV said, "*Et tu, Brute*? Will you stab Caesar, too?"

"*Et tu, Brute?*" is Latin for "You, too, Brutus?" Julius Caesar said these words to Brutus, whom he thought was his friend, when Brutus, with many other Romans, stabbed him to death.

Edward IV ordered, "Call a parley, sir, to Duke George of Clarence."

The trumpet sounded, requesting a parley.

Duke Richard of Gloucester and Duke George of Clarence talked together.

The Earl of Warwick called, "Come, Clarence, come; you will, if Warwick calls for you to."

Duke George of Clarence replied, "Father-in-law Warwick, do you know what this means?"

He took the red rose — symbol of the House of Lancaster — out of his hat and threw it toward the Earl of Warwick. Duke George of Clarence had been reconciled to his brother the King; once more, he was a Yorkist. He placed a white rose — symbol of the House of York — in his hat.

He continued, "Look here, I throw my infamy at you. I will not ruin my father's House — his family — by giving blood to cement the stones together and set up Lancaster.

"Do you think, Warwick, that Clarence is so harsh, so blunt, and so unnatural as to bend the fatal instruments of war against his brother and his lawful King?

"Perhaps you will raise as an objection my holy oath. To keep that oath would be more impious than Jephthah keeping his oath, when he sacrificed his daughter."

In Judges 11, Jephthah had vowed to sacrifice the first thing that came out of the door of his house when he returned home if God would grant him a military victory; unfortunately, the first thing to come out of the door was his only child: a daughter, whom he sacrificed.

Judges 11:30-34 (1599 Geneva Bible) states this:

"30 *And Jephthah vowed a vow unto the Lord, and said, If thou shalt deliver the children of Ammon into mine hands,*

"31 *Then that thing that cometh out of the doors of mine house to meet me, when I come home in peace from the children of Ammon, shall be the Lord's, and I will offer it for a burnt offering.*

"32 *And so Jephthah went unto the children of Ammon to fight against them, and the Lord delivered them into his hands.*

"33 *And he smote them from Aroer even till thou come to Minnith, twenty cities, and so forth to Abel of the vineyards, with an exceeding great slaughter. Thus the children of Ammon were humbled before the children of Israel.*

"34 *Now when Jephthah came to Mizpah unto his house, behold, his daughter came out to meet him with timbrels and dances, which was his only child: he had none other son, nor daughter.*"

Duke George of Clarence continued, "I am so sorry for the trespass I made that, to deserve well at my brother's hands, I here proclaim myself your mortal foe, and I resolve that wherever I meet you — and I will meet you, if you stir abroad — to plague you for foully misleading me.

"And so, proud-hearted Warwick, I defy you, and to my brother I turn my blushing cheeks.

"Pardon me, Edward. I will make amends.

"And, Richard, do not frown upon my faults, for I will henceforth be no more inconstant and disloyal."

King Edward IV said to him, "Now you are more welcome, and ten times more beloved, than if you had never deserved our hate."

Duke Richard of Gloucester said, "Welcome, good Clarence; this is brotherlike."

The Earl of Warwick said, "Oh, unsurpassed traitor; you are perjured and unjust!"

King Edward IV said, "Warwick, will you leave the town and fight? Or shall we beat the stones about your ears?"

The Earl of Warwick said, "Unfortunately for you, I am not cooped up here for defense! I will leave and go towards Barnet immediately, and I challenge you to battle me there, Edward, if you dare."

King Edward IV replied, "Yes, Warwick, Edward dares, and he leads the way.

"Lords, let's go to the battlefield! Saint George and victory!"

King Edward IV and his troops marched to the battlefield. The Earl of Warwick and his troops followed.

On 14 April 1471, the Battle of Barnet was being fought on a battlefield near Barnet. King Edward IV met the Earl of Warwick, who was mortally wounded and whose eyesight was failing.

King Edward IV said to him, "So, lie there. Die, you, and with you die our fear, for Warwick was a terror who frightened us all.

"Now, Marquess of Montague, sit fast, I seek you, so that Warwick's bones may keep your bones company."

King Edward IV exited.

Alone, the blinded Earl of Warwick said, "Who is near? Come to me, friend or foe, and tell me which General is the victor: York or Warwick?

"But why do I ask that? My mangled body shows, my blood shows, my lack of strength shows, my sick heart shows that I must yield my body to the earth, and by my fall, I must yield the victory to my foe.

"Thus yields the cedar to the axe's edge, although the cedar's arms gave shelter to the Princely eagle, and although under the cedar's shade the ramping lion slept, and although the cedar's topmost branch peered over Jove's spreading oak tree and protected low shrubs from winter's powerful wind.

"These eyes, which now are dimmed with death's black veil, have been as piercing as the mid-day Sun as they perceived the secret treasons of the world.

"The wrinkles in my brows, now filled with blood, were often likened to Kingly sepulchers, for who lived as King, except a person whose grave I could dig?

"And who dared to smile when Warwick frowned?

"But look, now my glory is smeared in dust and blood! My hunting grounds, my walks, my manors that I had just now have forsaken me, and of all my lands there is nothing left to me except my body's length — land enough for a grave.

"Why, pomp, rule, and reign are nothing but earth and dust! And, live us how we can, yet die we must."

The Earl of Oxford and the Duke of Somerset arrived.

The Duke of Somerset said, "Ah, Warwick, Warwick! If you were still uninjured, like us, we might recover all our losses. Queen Margaret has brought from France a powerful army. Just now we heard the news. I wish that you could flee!"

"Why, even if I could, I would not flee," Warwick said. "Ah, Marquess of Montague, if you are there, sweet brother, take my hand and with your lips kiss me and keep my soul in my body awhile! Your kiss will keep my soul from exiting my body through my lips. You don't love me because, brother, if you did, your tears would wash this cold, congealed blood that glues my lips and will not let me speak. Come quickly, Montague, or I will be dead before you get here."

The Duke of Somerset said, "Warwick, the Marquess of Montague has breathed his last, and to the last gasp he cried out for Warwick and said, 'Commend me to my valiant brother.' And he would have said more, and he did speak more that sounded like a clamor in a vault that could not be understood, but at last I heard him say clearly, delivered with a groan, 'Oh, farewell, Warwick!'"

The Earl of Warwick said, "May his soul sweetly rest! Flee, lords, and save yourselves, for Warwick bids you all farewell until we meet in Heaven."

He died.

The Earl of Oxford said, "Let's go, so we can meet the Queen's great army!"

— 5.3 —

On another part of the battlefield, King Edward IV celebrated his victory. With him were his brothers Duke Richard of Gloucester and Duke George of Clarence. Also present were many soldiers.

King Edward IV said, "Thus far our fortune keeps an upward course, and we are graced with wreaths of victory. But, in the midst of this brightly shining day, I spy a black, suspicious, threatening cloud that will battle our glorious Sun before it attains its easeful, comfortable western bed. I mean, my lords, those troops whom Queen Margaret has raised in France have arrived at our coast and, so we hear, march on to fight us."

Duke George of Clarence said, "A little gale will soon disperse that cloud and blow it to the source from whence it came. The very beams of the Sun will dry those vapors up, for not every cloud generates a storm."

Duke Richard of Gloucester said, "The Queen's forces are estimated to be thirty thousand strong, and both the Duke of Somerset and the Earl of Oxford have fled to her. If she is given time before she has to fight, be well assured that her faction will be fully as strong as ours."

King Edward IV said, "We are informed by our loving friends that Queen Margaret and her troops hold their course toward Tewksbury. We, having now the victory at Barnet battlefield, will go to Tewksbury immediately, for willingness makes for progress on the journey. And as we march, our strength will be augmented in every county as we go along."

He ordered the drummer, "Strike up the drum," and then he ordered everyone, "Cry 'Courage!' and let's go."

On the plains near Tewksbury, Queen Margaret, Prince Edward, the Duke of Somerset, and the Earl of Oxford were meeting. With them were many soldiers.

Queen Margaret said, "Great lords, wise men never sit and bewail their loss, but cheerfully seek how to repair their misfortunes.

"What though the mast is now blown overboard, the cable broken, the holding-anchor lost, and half our sailors swallowed in the flood? Our pilot — King Henry VI — still lives.

"Is it suitable that a pilot should leave the helm and like a fearful lad with tearful eyes add water to the sea and give more strength to that which has too much, while as he moans the rock splits the ship, which toil and courage might have saved?

"What a shame, what a fault that would be!

"Say Warwick was our anchor — what of that? And the Marquess of Montague was our topmost sail — what of him? Our slaughtered friends were the ship's tackles — what of these?

"Why, isn't Oxford here another anchor? And Somerset another goodly mast? The friends from France our sail-ropes and tacklings?

"And, although we are unskillful, why shouldn't my son Ned — Prince Edward — and I for once be allowed to perform the skillful pilot's duty?

"We will not leave the helm in order to sit and weep, but we will instead keep our course, although the rough wind says no, and we will avoid the sandbanks, shoals, and rocks that threaten us with wreck.

"It is as good to scold the waves as to speak well of them. And what is Edward but ruthless sea? What is Clarence but a quicksand of deceit? And what is Richard but a jagged, deadly rock?

"All these are enemies to our poor ship.

"Say you can swim — but you can swim only for a while! Tread on the quicksand; why, there you quickly sink. Bestride the rock; the tide will wash you off, or else you will starve. That's a threefold death: You can drown in the sea, sink in quicksand, or die of starvation on a rock.

"This speak I, lords, to let you understand, in case one of you would flee away from us, that there's no hoped-for mercy coming from the brothers —

Edward, Clarence, and Richard — no more than the mercy you would get from the ruthless waves, quicksand, and rocks.

"Why, be courageous then! It is childish weakness to lament or fear what cannot be avoided."

Prince Edward said, "I think a woman of this valiant spirit would, if a coward heard her speak these words, infuse his breast with greatness of heart and nobleness of spirit and make him, without armor and weapons, defeat an armed warrior.

"I don't say this because I doubt the courage of anyone here, for if I did suspect a man to be fearful he would have my permission to go away right now, lest when we need him to fight he might infect another man and make him of similar fearful spirit as himself.

"If any such be here — God forbid! — let him depart before we need his help."

The Earl of Oxford said, "Women and children have so high a courage — and warriors are faint-hearted! Why, for warriors to have faint hearts is perpetual shame.

"Oh, brave young Prince! Your famous grandfather — King Henry V — lives again in you. Long may you live to bear his image and renew his glories!"

The Duke of Somerset said, "And may he who will not fight for such a hope as the young Prince go home to bed, and like an owl that is seen during the day, be mocked and wondered at if he arise."

Queen Margaret said, "Thanks, gentle Somerset; sweet Oxford, thanks."

Prince Edward said, "And take thanks from me, who as of yet has nothing else to give you."

A messenger arrived and said, "Prepare yourselves, lords, for Edward IV is at hand and ready to fight; therefore, be resolute."

The Earl of Oxford said, "I thought no less. It is his military strategy to hasten so quickly in order to find us unprepared to fight."

"But he's deceived," the Duke of Somerset said. "We are ready to fight."

"Seeing your eagerness to fight cheers my heart," Queen Margaret said.

"Here we will pitch our battle formation," the Earl of Oxford said. "From here we will not budge."

King Edward IV, Duke Richard of Gloucester, Duke George of Clarence, and many soldiers arrived.

King Edward IV said, "Brave followers, yonder stands the metaphorical thorny wood, which by the Heavens' assistance and your strength must by the roots be hewn up before night. I need not add more fuel to your fire, for well I know you blaze to burn them out. Give the signal for the battle, and let's go to it, lords!"

Queen Margaret said, "Lords, knights, and gentlemen, my tears contradict what words I should say because as you see, for every word I speak I drink the water of my eyes. Therefore, I will say no more but this: Henry VI, your sovereign, is held prisoner by the foe; his Kingship is usurped, his realm is a slaughterhouse, his subjects are being slain, his laws and statutes are cancelled, and his treasure is spent. And yonder is the wolf that makes this spoil. Your fight is just, and so then, in God's name, lords, be valiant and give the signal for the battle."

The battle started.

The battle was over, and King Edward IV was triumphant. King Edward IV, Duke Richard of Gloucester, and Duke George of Clarence stood together with their prisoners: Queen Margaret, the Earl of Oxford, and the Duke of Somerset. Many Yorkist soldiers were present.

King Edward IV said, "Now here ends our tumultuous broils. Take the Earl of Oxford away to Hames Castle immediately. As for the Duke of Somerset, cut off his guilty head. Go, take them away; I will not hear them speak."

The Earl of Oxford said, "For my part, I'll not trouble you with words."

The Duke of Somerset said, "Nor will I, but I bow with patience to my ill fortune."

Queen Margaret said to the Earl of Oxford and the Duke of Somerset, "So part we sadly in this troublous world, but we will meet with joy in the sweet city of Jerusalem in Heaven."

Guards took away the Earl of Oxford and the Duke of Somerset.

King Edward IV said, "Has the proclamation been made that whoever finds Prince Edward, Queen Margaret's son, shall have a large reward, and Prince Edward shall keep his life?"

"The proclamation has been made," Duke Richard of Gloucester said, "and look, here comes the youthful Prince Edward!"

Soldiers arrived, bringing Prince Edward.

King Edward IV said, "Bring forth the gallant, and let us hear him speak. What! Can so young a thorn begin to prick? Prince Edward, what penalty can you pay for bearing arms, for stirring up my subjects to rebel against me, and for all the trouble you have caused me?"

Prince Edward replied, "Speak like a subject, proud ambitious York! Suppose that I am now my father's mouthpiece. Resign your throne, and where I stand kneel before me, while I say the same questions to you, traitor, which you would have me answer."

Queen Margaret said, "I wish that your father had been so resolute!"

Duke Richard of Gloucester said, "If he had been, then you might always have worn the petticoat, and never have stolen the pants from your husband, Henry VI, and worn them."

Prince Edward said, "Let Aesop tell false fables during a winter's night; Richard's currish riddles are not suitable for this place."

Aesop was popularly supposed to be hunchbacked like Richard. The word "currish" meant "like a cur, aka a mean-spirited dog."

Duke Richard of Gloucester said, "By Heaven, brat, I'll plague you for that word."

Queen Margaret said, "True, you were born to be a plague to men."

"For God's sake, take away this captive scold," Duke Richard of Gloucester said.

"No," Prince Edward said. "Instead, take away this scolding hunchback."

"Be quiet, willful boy, or I will put a charm on your tongue to make it silent," King Edward IV said.

"Untutored, badly raised lad, you are too malapert and impudent," Duke George of Clarence said.

"I know my duty," Prince Edward said. "You are all undutiful. Lascivious Edward, and you perjured George, and you misshapen Dick, I tell you all that I am your better, traitors as you are, and you have usurped my father's right and mine."

King Edward IV stabbed Prince Edward and said, "Take that, you likeness of this railer — Queen Margaret — here."

Duke Richard of Gloucester stabbed Prince Edward and said, "Are you suffering your death throes? Take that, to end your agony."

Duke George of Clarence stabbed Prince Edward and said, "And this is for twitting me with perjury."

Prince Edward died.

Queen Margaret said, "Oh, kill me, too!"

"By Mother Mary, I shall," Duke Richard of Gloucester said.

King Edward IV stopped him by saying, "Don't, Richard, don't; for we have already done too much."

Duke Richard of Gloucester asked, "Why should Queen Margaret live? She will fill the world with words."

Queen Margaret fainted.

King Edward IV said, "Does she swoon? Help her."

During the commotion, Duke Richard of Gloucester said quietly to his brother Duke George of Clarence, "Clarence, excuse me to the King my brother. I'll leave here and go to London on a serious matter. Before you come there, you will be sure to hear some news."

"What? What?" Duke George of Clarence asked.

"The Tower! The Tower!" Duke Richard of Gloucester replied.

He exited.

Brought back to consciousness, Queen Margaret said, "Oh, Ned, sweet Ned! Speak to your mother, boy! Can't you speak?

"Oh, traitors! Murderers! They who stabbed Julius Caesar shed no blood at all, did not offend, and did not deserve blame, if this foul deed were nearby to be compared to it. Julius Caesar was a man; this, in comparison, is a child. And men never expend their fury on a child.

"What's worse than being a murderer, so that I may name it? No, no, my heart will burst, if I speak. And I will speak, so that my heart may burst. Butchers and villains! Bloody cannibals! How sweet a plant you have untimely cut!

"You have no children, butchers! If you had, the thought of them would have stirred up remorse. But if you ever chance to have a child, look in his youth to have him so cut off as, you deathmen and executioners, you have killed this sweet young Prince!"

King Edward IV said, "Take her away! Go and bear her forcibly away from here."

Queen Margaret said, "No, never carry me away from here; instead, kill me here and now. Here in my chest sheathe your sword; I'll pardon you for killing me. What, Edward IV, you will not? Then, Clarence, you do it."

"I swear by Heaven that I will not cause you so much comfort," Duke George of Clarence replied.

Queen Margaret said, "Good Clarence, do it; sweet Clarence, please do it."

"Didn't you hear me swear I would not do it?" Duke George of Clarence replied.

"Yes, I did, but you are used to committing perjury," Queen Margaret said. "Committing perjury was a sin before, but now it is a charitable deed. Won't you kill me?

"Where is that Devil's butcher, ugly Richard? Richard, where are you? You are not here. Murder is your good deed. You never refuse those who petition you to shed other people's blood."

King Edward IV ordered, "Take her away, I say; I order you, carry her away from here."

Queen Margaret said, "May what happened to my son the Prince happen to you and yours!"

Guards forcibly carried her away.

King Edward IV asked, "Where has Richard gone?"

Duke George of Clarence said, "To London, in all haste."

He thought, *And, I guess, to make a bloody supper in the Tower of London.*

King Edward IV said, "Richard acts quickly, if an idea comes into his head.

"Now we will march away from here. Discharge the common soldiers with pay and thanks, and let's go away to London and see how well our gentle Queen fares. By this time, I hope, she has given birth to a son for me."

King Henry VI and a Lieutenant were in a room of the Tower of London when Duke Richard of Gloucester arrived. King Henry VI was reading a religious book.

Duke Richard of Gloucester said, "Good day, my lord. Studying your book so hard?"

"Yes, my good lord," King Henry VI said. "I should say rather 'my lord' because it is a sin to flatter; 'good' is a 'little' better than you deserve and so it is flattery. 'Good Gloucester' and 'good Devil' are alike, and both are contrary to the way things should be; therefore, I ought not to call you 'good lord.'"

Duke Richard of Gloucester said to the Lieutenant, "Sirrah, leave us to ourselves. We must confer."

The Lieutenant exited.

King Henry VI, who suspected what was about to occur, and who may have had the gift of prophecy, said, "So flees the reckless shepherd from the wolf. So the harmless sheep first yields his fleece and next yields his throat to the butcher's knife. What scene of death has the famous Roman tragedian Roscius now to act? How am I to die?"

Duke Richard of Gloucester replied, "Suspicion always haunts the guilty mind. The thief is afraid that each bush is an officer of the law."

King Henry VI said, "After being trapped in a bush, with trembling wings a bird fears every bush. And I, the hapless father to one sweet bird, the Prince, now have the fatal object in my eye where my poor young bird was trapped, caught, and killed. I need not fear every bush because in front of me I see the bush that I ought to fear."

Duke Richard of Gloucester said, "Why, what a peevish fool was that father of Crete, who taught his son the function of a foolish fowl! And yet, for all his wings, the fool was drowned."

He was referring to the myth of Daedalus and Icarus. Imprisoned by King Minos on the island of Crete, they escaped after Daedalus fashioned wings made of wax and feathers. Icarus, however, flew too close to the hot Sun, which melted the wax of his wings, and he fell into the sea and drowned.

King Henry VI said, "I am Daedalus; my poor boy is Icarus; your father, the old Duke of York, is King Minos, who would not allow us to freely leave Crete; the sun that seared the wings of my sweet boy is your brother Edward; and you yourself are the sea whose malicious whirlpool swallowed up my son's life. Ah, kill me with your weapon, not with words! My breast can better endure feeling your dagger's point than my ears can endure hearing that tragic history.

"But why have you come? Have you come to take my life?"

Duke Richard of Gloucester asked, "Do you think that I am an executioner?"

"I am sure you are a persecutor," King Henry VI said. "If murdering innocents is executing, why, then you are an executioner."

"I killed your son for his presumption," Duke Richard of Gloucester said.

"If you had been killed when you first presumed, then you would not have lived to kill a son of mine," King Henry VI said. "And thus I prophesy that many a thousand people, who now mistrust no part of what I fear, and many an old man's and many a widow's sigh, and many an orphan's tear-filled eye — men for their sons, wives for their husbands, and orphans for their parents' untimely death — shall bitterly regret the hour that you were born.

"The owl shrieked at your birth — an evil sign. The night-crow cried, foretelling a luckless time. Dogs howled, and a hideous tempest shook down trees. The raven crouched on the chimney's top, and chattering magpies sang dismal discords.

"Your mother felt more than a mother's pain of childbirth, and yet brought forth less than a mother's hope. I mean that she gave birth to an incomplete and deformed lump, not like the fruit expected from such a splendid tree as your mother.

"You had teeth in your head when you were born to signify that you came to bite the world. And, if the rest be true that I have heard, you came —"

"I'll hear no more," Duke Richard of Gloucester said. "Die, prophet, in the middle of your speech."

He stabbed King Henry VI and said, "For this deed among the rest of my deeds, I was ordained. For such deeds I was born."

"Yes, and for much more slaughter after this," King Henry VI said.

As he died, King Henry VI said, "May God forgive my sins, and may God pardon you!"

Duke Richard of Gloucester said over King Henry VI's corpse, "Will the ambitious, soaring blood of Lancaster sink into the ground? I thought it would have mounted into the sky. See how my sword weeps for the poor King's death! Oh, may such bloody tears be always shed from those who wish the downfall of our House of York!

"If any spark of life is yet remaining, go down, down to Hell — and say I sent you there."

Duke Richard of Gloucester stabbed King Henry VI's corpse.

He continued, "I, who haven't pity, love, or fear, sent you there. Indeed, what Henry VI told me is true, for I have often heard my mother say that I came into the world with my legs and feet first. Didn't I have reason, you think, to make haste and seek the ruin of those who usurped our right? The midwife wondered and the women cried, 'Oh, Jesus bless us, he is born with teeth!' And so I was, which plainly signified that I would snarl and bite and play the mean dog.

"So then, since the Heavens have misshaped my body, let Hell make my mind crooked to correspond to my crooked body.

"I have no brother, I am like no brother, and this word 'love,' which graybeards call divine, is resident in men who are like one another, but it is not resident in me: I am myself alone.

"Clarence, beware, for you are keeping me from the light, from my golden-crowned goal. But I will arrange a pitch-black day for you, for I will buzz abroad rumors of such prophecies that Edward IV shall fear for his life, and then, to purge his fear by lancing and bloodletting, I'll be your death.

"King Henry VI and his son — the Prince — are dead and gone. Clarence, your turn is next, and then the rest who are in line ahead of me to be King of England. I regard myself as worthless until I am the best and highest-ranking person in England.

"I'll throw your body in another room and triumph, Henry VI, in your day of doom."

In a room of the palace in London were King Edward IV, Queen Elizabeth, Duke George of Clarence, Duke Richard of Gloucester, Lord Hastings, a nurse holding the recently born Prince, and some attendants.

Using the royal plural, King Edward IV said, "Once more we sit on England's royal throne, repurchased with the blood of enemies. What valiant foemen, similar to autumn's wheat, have we mown down, at the peak of all their pride!

"We have mown down three Dukes of Somerset, who were threefold renowned as hardy and undoubted champions; two Cliffords, both the father and the son; and two Northumberlands — two braver men never spurred their warhorses at the military trumpet's sound.

"Along with them, we have mown down the two brave bears, Warwick and Montague, who in their chains fettered the Kingly lion and made the forest tremble when they roared."

The Earl of Warwick, the Marquess of Montague, and the Earl of Warwick's father were members of the Neville family, whose crest depicted a rampant — standing — bear chained to a knobby post.

King Edward IV continued, "Thus have we swept suspicion and anxiety from our seat and made our footstool out of security."

King Edward IV thought that he was safe and secure on the throne, but already Duke Richard of Gloucester was plotting to become King of England. A now rare meaning of "security" is "overconfidence."

He continued, "Come here, Bess — my Queen — and let me kiss my boy.

"Young Ned, your uncles and I have in our armors stayed awake during the winter's night and gone on foot in the summer's scalding heat, so that you could possess the crown in peace and so that you shall reap the gain of our labors."

Duke Richard of Gloucester thought, *I'll blast your son's harvest, if your head were laid in the grave, the way that a storm can blight a harvest by driving the tops of the wheat into the ground, for I am not yet respected in the world. This shoulder of mine was created so thick so that it could heave, and it shall either heave some bodies out of my way, or break my back.*

He touched his head and thought, *You work out the way to accomplish my goals.*

Then he touched his shoulder and thought, *And you shall execute the plan.*

King Edward IV continued, "Clarence and Gloucester, love my lovely Queen, and kiss your Princely nephew, both of you brothers of mine."

Duke George of Clarence said, "The duty that I owe to your majesty I seal upon the lips of this sweet babe."

"Thanks, noble Clarence," Queen Elizabeth said, "Worthy brother, thanks."

Duke Richard of Gloucester said, "And, because I love the tree from whence this babe sprang, witness the loving kiss I give the fruit."

He kissed the recently born Prince and thought, *And Judas cried 'all hail!' when he meant all harm.*

Judas betrayed Jesus with a kiss.

Matthew 26:48-49 states, "*Now he that betrayed him, had given them a token, saying, Whomsoever I shall kiss, that is he, lay hold on him. And forthwith he came to Jesus, and said, God save thee, Master, and kissed him*" (1599 Geneva Bible).

King Edward IV said, "Now am I seated as my soul delights because I have my country's peace and my brothers' loves."

Duke George of Clarence said, "What does your grace want to do with Queen Margaret? Reignier, her father, has pawned Sicily, Naples, and Jerusalem to the King of France and has sent here the money raised for her ransom."

"Send her away, and waft her over the sea to France," King Edward IV said. "And what remains to be done now but that we spend the time with stately triumphs and mirthful comic shows such as are suitable for the pleasure of the court?

"Sound, drums and trumpets!

"Farewell, sour, bitter annoyances! For here, I hope, begins our lasting joy."

Appendix A: Brief Historical Background

KING EDWARD I: 1272-1307

Edward Longshanks fought and defeated the Welsh chieftains, and he made his eldest son the Prince of Wales. He won victories against the Scots, and he brought the coronation stone from Scone to Westminster.

KING EDWARD II: 1307-deposed 1327

At the Battle of Bannockburn in 1314, the Scots defeated his army. His wife and her lover, Mortimer, deposed him. According to legend, he was murdered in Berkeley Castle by means of a red-hot poker thrust up his anus.

KING EDWARD III: 1327-1377

Son of King Edward II, he reigned for a long time — 50 years. Because he wanted to conquer Scotland and France, he started the Hundred Years War in 1338. King Edward III and his eldest son, Edward the Black Prince, won important victories against the French in the Battle of Crécy (1346) and the Battle of Poitiers (1356).

One of King Edward III's sons was John of Gaunt, first Duke of Lancaster.

Another of King Edward III's sons was Edmund of Langley, first Duke of York.

During his reign, the Black Death — the bubonic plague — struck in 1348-1350 and killed half of England's population.

KING RICHARD II: 1377-deposed 1399

King Richard II was the son of Edward the Black Prince. In 1381, Wat Tyler led the Peasants Revolt, which was suppressed. King Richard II sent Henry, Duke of Lancaster, into exile and seized Henry's estates, but in 1399 Henry, Duke of Lancaster, returned from exile and deposed King Richard II, thereby becoming King Henry IV. In 1400, King Richard II was murdered in Pontefract Castle, which is also known as Pomfret Castle.

HOUSE OF LANCASTER

KING HENRY IV: 1399-1413

Henry, Duke of Lancaster, was the son of John of Gaunt, who was the third son of King Edward III. He was born at Bolingbroke Castle and so was also known as Henry of Bolingbroke. Returning from exile in France to reclaim his estates, he deposed King Richard II. He spent the 13 years of his reign putting down rebellions and defending himself against those who would assassinate or depose him. The Welshman Owen Glendower and the English Percy family were among those who fought against him. King Henry IV died at the age of 45.

KING HENRY V: 1413-1422

The son of King Henry IV, King Henry V renewed the war with France. He and his army defeated the French at the Battle of Agincourt (1415) despite being heavily outnumbered. He married Catherine of Valoise, the daughter of the French King, but he died before becoming King of France. He left behind a 10-month-old son, who became King Henry VI.

KING HENRY VI: 1422-deposed 1461; briefly returned to the throne in 1470-1471

The Hundred Years War ended in 1453; the English lost all land in France except for Calais, a port city. After King Henry VI suffered an attack of mental illness in 1454, Richard, third Duke of York and the father of King Henry IV and King Richard III, was made Protector of the Realm. England suffered civil war after the House of York challenged King Henry VI's right to be King of England. In 1470, King Henry VI was briefly restored to the English throne. In 1471, he was murdered in the Tower of London. A short time previously, his son, Edward, Prince of Wales, had been killed at the Battle of Tewkesbury in 1471; this was the final battle in the Wars of the Roses. The Yorkists decisively defeated the Lancastrians.

King Henry VI founded both Eton College and King's College, Cambridge.

WARS OF THE ROSES

From 1455-1487, the Yorkists and the Lancastrians fought for power in England in the famous Wars of the Roses. The emblem of the York family was a white rose, and the emblem of the Lancaster family was a red rose. The Yorkists and the Lancastrians were descended from King Edward III.

HOUSE OF YORK

KING EDWARD IV: 1461-1483 (King Henry VI briefly returned to the throne in 1470-1471)

Son of Richard, third Duke of York, he charged his brother George, Duke of Clarence, with treason and had him murdered in 1478. After dying suddenly, he left behind two sons aged 12 and 9, and five daughters.

His surviving two brothers in Shakespeare's play *Richard III* are these: 1) George, Duke of Clarence. Clarence is the second-oldest brother; and 2) Richard, Duke of Gloucester, and afterwards King Richard III. Gloucester is the youngest surviving brother.

William Caxton established the first printing press in Westminster during King Edward IV's reign.

KING EDWARD V: 1483-1483

The eldest son of King Edward IV, he reigned for only two months, the shortest-lived monarch in English history. He was 13 years old. He and his younger brother, Richard, were murdered in the Tower of London. According to Shakespeare's play, their uncle, Richard, Duke of Gloucester, who became King Richard III, was responsible for their murders.

KING RICHARD III: 1483-1485

Brother of King Edward IV, Richard, the Duke of Gloucester, declared the two Princes in the Tower of London — King Edward V and Richard, Duke of York — illegitimate and made himself King Richard III. In 1485, Henry Tudor, Earl of Richmond, a descendant of John of Gaunt, who was the father of King Henry IV, defeated King Richard III at the Battle of Bosworth Field in Leicestershire. King Richard III died in that battle.

King Richard III's father was Richard Plantagenet, Duke of York. His mother was Cecily Neville, Duchess of York.

King Richard III's death in the Battle of Bosworth Field is regarded as marking the end of the Middle Ages in England.

A NOTE ON THE PLANTAGENETS

The first Plantagenet King was King Henry II (1154-1189). From 1154 until 1485, when King Richard III died, all English Kings were Plantagenets. Both the Lancaster family and the York family were Plantagenets.

Geoffrey Plantagenet, Count of Anjou, was the founder of the House of Plantagenet. Geoffrey's son, Henry Curtmantle, became King Henry II of England, thereby founding the Plantagenet dynasty. Geoffrey wore a sprig of broom, a flowering shrub, as a badge; the Latin name for broom is *planta genista*, and from it the name "Plantagenet" arose.

The Plantagenet dynasty can be divided into three parts:

1154-1216: The Angevins. The Angevin Kings were Henry II, Richard I (Richard the Lionheart), and John 1.

1216-1399: The Plantagenets. These Kings ranged from King Henry III to King Richard II.

1399-1485: The Houses of Lancaster and of York. These Kings ranged from King Henry IV to King Richard III.

BEGINNING OF THE TUDOR DYNASTY

KING HENRY VII: 1485-1509

When King Richard III fell at the Battle of Bosworth, Henry Tudor, Earl of Richmond, became King Henry VII. A Lancastrian, he married Elizabeth of York — young Elizabeth of York in *Richard III* — and united the two warring houses, York and Lancaster, thus ending the Wars of the Roses. One of his grandfathers was Sir Owen Tudor, who married Catherine of Valoise, widow of King Henry V.

KING HENRY VIII: 1509-1547

King Henry VIII had six wives. These are their fates: "Divorced, Beheaded, Died, Divorced, Beheaded, Survived." He divorced his first wife, Catherine of Aragon, so that he could marry Anne Boleyn. Because of this, England divorced itself from the Catholic Church, and King Henry VIII became the head of the Church of England. King Henry VIII had one son and two daughters, all of whom became rulers of England: Edward, daughter of Jane Seymour; Mary, daughter of Catherine of Aragon; and Elizabeth, daughter of Anne Boleyn.

KING EDWARD VI: 1547-1553

The son of Henry VIII and Jane Seymour, King Edward VI succeeded his father at the age of nine; a Council of Regency with his uncle, Duke of Somerset, styled Protector, ruled the government.

During King Edward VI's reign, Archbishop Thomas Cranmer wrote the 1549 Book of Common Prayer.

When King Edward VI died, Lady Jane Grey was proclaimed Queen, but she ruled for only nine days before being executed in 1554, aged 17. Mary, daughter of Catherine of Aragon, became Queen. She was Catholic, thus the attempt to make Lady Jane Grey, a Protestant, Queen.

QUEEN MARY I (BLOODY MARY) 1553-1558

Queen Mary I attempted to make England a Catholic nation again. Some Protestant bishops, including Archbishop Thomas Cranmer, were burnt at the stake, and other violence broke out, resulting in her being known as Bloody Mary.

QUEEN ELIZABETH I: 1558-1603

The daughter of King Henry VIII and Anne Boleyn, Queen Elizabeth I was a popular Queen. In 1588, the English navy decisively defeated the Spanish Armada. England had many notable playwrights and poets, including William Shakespeare and Ben Jonson, during her reign. She never married and had no children.

KING JAMES I OF ENGLAND: A MEMBER OF THE HOUSE OF STUART

KING JAMES I OF ENGLAND AND VI OF SCOTLAND: 1603-1625

King James I of England was the son of Mary, Queen of Scots, and Lord Darnley. In 1605 Guy Fawkes and his Catholic co-conspirators were captured before they could blow up the Houses of Parliament; this was known as the Gunpowder Plot.

In 1611, during King James I's reign, the Authorized Version of the Bible (the King James Version) was completed.

Also during King James I's reign, in 1620 the Pilgrims sailed for America in their ship *The Mayflower*.

A NOTE ON SHAKESPEARE

William Shakespeare lived under two monarchs: Queen Elizabeth I and King James I.

Appendix B: About the Author

It was a dark and stormy night. Suddenly a cry rang out, and on a hot summer night in 1954, Josephine, wife of Carl Bruce, gave birth to a boy — me. Unfortunately, this young married couple allowed Reuben Saturday, Josephine's brother, to name their first-born. Reuben, aka "The Joker," decided that Bruce was a nice name, so he decided to name me Bruce Bruce. I have gone by my middle name — David — ever since.

Being named Bruce David Bruce hasn't been all bad. Bank tellers remember me very quickly, so I don't often have to show an ID. It can be fun in charades, also. When I was a counselor as a teenager at Camp Echoing Hills in Warsaw, Ohio, a fellow counselor gave the signs for "sounds like" and "two words," then she pointed to a bruise on her leg twice. Bruise Bruise? Oh yeah, Bruce Bruce is the answer!

Uncle Reuben, by the way, gave me a haircut when I was in kindergarten. He cut my hair short and shaved a small bald spot on the back of my head. My mother wouldn't let me go to school until the bald spot grew out again.

Of all my brothers and sisters (six in all), I am the only transplant to Athens, Ohio. I was born in Newark, Ohio, and have lived all around Southeastern Ohio. However, I moved to Athens to go to Ohio University and have never left.

At Ohio U, I never could make up my mind whether to major in English or Philosophy, so I got a bachelor's degree with a double major in both areas, then I added a master's degree in English and a master's degree in Philosophy.

Currently, and for a long time to come (I eat fruits and veggies), I am spending my retirement writing books such as *Nadia Comaneci: Perfect 10*, *The Funniest People in Dance*, *Homer's* Iliad: *A Retelling in Prose*, and *William Shakespeare's* Othello: *A Retelling in Prose*.

By the way, my sister Brenda Kennedy writes romances such as *A New Beginning* and *Shattered Dreams*.

Appendix C: Some Books by David Bruce

Retellings of a Classic Work of Literature

Arden of Faversham*: A Retelling*

Ben Jonson's The Alchemist: *A Retelling*

Ben Jonson's The Arraignment, or Poetaster: *A Retelling*

Ben Jonson's Bartholomew Fair: *A Retelling*

Ben Jonson's The Case is Altered: *A Retelling*

Ben Jonson's Catiline's Conspiracy: *A Retelling*

Ben Jonson's The Devil is an Ass: *A Retelling*

Ben Jonson's Epicene: *A Retelling*

Ben Jonson's Every Man in His Humor: *A Retelling*

Ben Jonson's Every Man Out of His Humor: *A Retelling*

Ben Jonson's The Fountain of Self-Love, or Cynthia's Revels: *A Retelling*

Ben Jonson's The Magnetic Lady, or Humors Reconciled: *A Retelling*

Ben Jonson's The New Inn, or The Light Heart: *A Retelling*

Ben Jonson's Sejanus' Fall: *A Retelling*

Ben Jonson's The Staple of News: *A Retelling*

Ben Jonson's A Tale of a Tub: *A Retelling*

Ben Jonson's Volpone, or the Fox: *A Retelling*

Christopher Marlowe's Complete Plays: Retellings

Christopher Marlowe's Dido, Queen of Carthage: *A Retelling*

Christopher Marlowe's Doctor Faustus: *Retellings of the 1604 A-Text and of the 1616 B-Text*

Christopher Marlowe's Edward II: *A Retelling*

Christopher Marlowe's The Massacre at Paris: *A Retelling*

Christopher Marlowe's The Rich Jew of Malta: *A Retelling*

Christopher Marlowe's Tamburlaine, Parts 1 and 2: *Retellings*

Dante's Divine Comedy: *A Retelling in Prose*

Dante's Inferno: *A Retelling in Prose*

Dante's Purgatory: *A Retelling in Prose*

Dante's Paradise: *A Retelling in Prose*

The Famous Victories of Henry V: *A Retelling*

From the Iliad *to the* Odyssey: *A Retelling in Prose of Quintus of Smyrna's* Posthomerica

George Chapman, Ben Jonson, and John Marston's Eastward Ho! *A Retelling*

George Peele's The Arraignment of Paris: *A Retelling*

George Peele's The Battle of Alcazar: *A Retelling*

George Peele's David and Bathsheba, and the Tragedy of Absalom: *A Retelling*

George Peele's Edward I: *A Retelling*

George Peele's The Old Wives' Tale: *A Retelling*

George-a-Greene: *A Retelling*

The History of King Leir: *A Retelling*

Homer's Iliad: *A Retelling in Prose*

Homer's Odyssey: *A Retelling in Prose*

J.W. Gent.'s The Valiant Scot: *A Retelling*

Jason and the Argonauts: A Retelling in Prose of Apollonius of Rhodes' Argonautica

John Ford: Eight Plays Translated into Modern English

John Ford's The Broken Heart: *A Retelling*

John Ford's The Fancies, Chaste and Noble: *A Retelling*

John Ford's The Lady's Trial: *A Retelling*

John Ford's The Lover's Melancholy: *A Retelling*

John Ford's Love's Sacrifice: *A Retelling*

John Ford's Perkin Warbeck: *A Retelling*

John Ford's The Queen: *A Retelling*

John Ford's 'Tis Pity She's a Whore: *A Retelling*

John Lyly's Campaspe: *A Retelling*

John Lyly's Endymion, The Man in the Moon: *A Retelling*

John Lyly's Galatea: *A Retelling*

John Lyly's Love's Metamorphosis: *A Retelling*

John Lyly's Midas: *A Retelling*

John Lyly's Mother Bombie: *A Retelling*

John Lyly's Sappho and Phao: *A Retelling*

John Lyly's The Woman in the Moon: *A Retelling*

John Webster's The White Devil: *A Retelling*

King Edward III: *A Retelling*

Mankind: *A Medieval Morality Play* (A Retelling)

Margaret Cavendish's The Unnatural Tragedy: *A Retelling*

The Merry Devil of Edmonton: A Retelling

The Summoning of Everyman: A Medieval Morality Play (A Retelling)

Robert Greene's Friar Bacon and Friar Bungay: *A Retelling*

The Taming of a Shrew: A Retelling

Tarlton's Jests: A Retelling

Thomas Middleton's A Chaste Maid in Cheapside: *A Retelling*

Thomas Middleton's Women Beware Women: *A Retelling*

Thomas Middleton and Thomas Dekker's The Roaring Girl: *A Retelling*

Thomas Middleton and William Rowley's The Changeling: *A Retelling*

The Trojan War and Its Aftermath: Four Ancient Epic Poems

Virgil's Aeneid: *A Retelling in Prose*

William Shakespeare's 5 Late Romances: Retellings in Prose

William Shakespeare's 10 Histories: Retellings in Prose

William Shakespeare's 11 Tragedies: Retellings in Prose

William Shakespeare's 12 Comedies: Retellings in Prose

William Shakespeare's 38 Plays: Retellings in Prose

William Shakespeare's 1 Henry IV, aka Henry IV, Part 1: *A Retelling in Prose*

William Shakespeare's 2 Henry IV, aka Henry IV, Part 2: *A Retelling in Prose*
William Shakespeare's 1 Henry VI, aka Henry VI, Part 1: *A Retelling in Prose*
William Shakespeare's 2 Henry VI, aka Henry VI, Part 2: *A Retelling in Prose*
William Shakespeare's 3 Henry VI, aka Henry VI, Part 3: *A Retelling in Prose*
William Shakespeare's All's Well that Ends Well: *A Retelling in Prose*
William Shakespeare's Antony and Cleopatra: *A Retelling in Prose*
William Shakespeare's As You Like It: *A Retelling in Prose*
William Shakespeare's The Comedy of Errors: *A Retelling in Prose*
William Shakespeare's Coriolanus: *A Retelling in Prose*
William Shakespeare's Cymbeline: *A Retelling in Prose*
William Shakespeare's Hamlet: *A Retelling in Prose*
William Shakespeare's Henry V: *A Retelling in Prose*
William Shakespeare's Henry VIII: *A Retelling in Prose*
William Shakespeare's Julius Caesar: *A Retelling in Prose*
William Shakespeare's King John: *A Retelling in Prose*
William Shakespeare's King Lear: *A Retelling in Prose*
William Shakespeare's Love's Labor's Lost: *A Retelling in Prose*
William Shakespeare's Macbeth: *A Retelling in Prose*
William Shakespeare's Measure for Measure: *A Retelling in Prose*
William Shakespeare's The Merchant of Venice: *A Retelling in Prose*
William Shakespeare's The Merry Wives of Windsor: *A Retelling in Prose*
William Shakespeare's A Midsummer Night's Dream: *A Retelling in Prose*
William Shakespeare's Much Ado About Nothing: *A Retelling in Prose*
William Shakespeare's Othello: *A Retelling in Prose*
William Shakespeare's Pericles, Prince of Tyre: *A Retelling in Prose*
William Shakespeare's Richard II: *A Retelling in Prose*
William Shakespeare's Richard III: *A Retelling in Prose*
William Shakespeare's Romeo and Juliet: *A Retelling in Prose*
William Shakespeare's The Taming of the Shrew: *A Retelling in Prose*
William Shakespeare's The Tempest: *A Retelling in Prose*
William Shakespeare's Timon of Athens: *A Retelling in Prose*
William Shakespeare's Titus Andronicus: *A Retelling in Prose*
William Shakespeare's Troilus and Cressida: *A Retelling in Prose*
William Shakespeare's Twelfth Night: *A Retelling in Prose*
William Shakespeare's The Two Gentlemen of Verona: *A Retelling in Prose*
William Shakespeare's The Two Noble Kinsmen: *A Retelling in Prose*
William Shakespeare's The Winter's Tale: *A Retelling in Prose*